Katherine floorboarded it and we took off after the green car, which had quite a head start. We had turned south on Main Street before I even got the door closed behind me. There was no traffic at that time of night and we could see the taillights of the green car several blocks ahead. Katherine concentrated on the car in front of us and stomped the pedal. The Cadillac skidded on the wet pavement but she jerked the wheel and got it back under control. Gael reached under her seat and pulled out a sawed-off shotgun as casually as though she were pulling out a fresh pack of cigarettes. Hell, I thought she had just been kidding earlier about having one. She cracked the gun and checked it for shells, gave a satisfied grunt, and nodded. She calmly rolled down the window and climbed out of it so she was sitting on the door with her head and body outside and just her legs in the car. She yelled for Katherine to hurry up and catch the jerks.

I leaned back in my seat and pulled out my pistol. I felt like Wyatt Earp getting ready for the O.K. Corral.

We were gaining on the car when something occurred to me. I leaned over the front seat and pulled Gael back inside the car. "What the hell are we doing? Those assholes have a machine gun!"

Bayou City Secrets

—A Hollis Carpenter Mystery by—

DEBORAH POWELL

The Naiad Press, Inc.
1991

Printed in the United States of America on acid-free paper
First Edition

Edited by Katherine V. Forrest
Cover design by Pat Tong and Bonnie Liss
(Phoenix Graphics)
Typeset by Sandi Stancil

Library of Congress Cataloging-in-Publication Data

Powell, Deborah, 1951—
Bayou city secrets / by Deborah Powell.
p. cm.
ISBN 0-941483-91-6 : $8.95
I. Title.
PS3566.0827B39 1991
813'.54--dc20 90-21908
CIP

To Mama and Daddy
for being funny

About the Author

Originally from Sunflower, Mississippi, Deborah Powell lives in Houston, Texas, with her lover and two dogs. *Bayou City Secrets* is her first novel. She is presently working on a sequel.

I felt great that morning leaving for work despite the unusually cold weather for Houston. The thermometer on the fence said twenty degrees but there was a strong wind out of the north and the day was damp. It felt more like twenty below.

I ran to my car, jumped in, grabbed my blanket and wrapped it around me, turned the key, flipped the switch, and stomped the starter button. The engine purred to life. I mashed the accelerator harder than necessary to feel the car jump forward. I had bought the car four months earlier in October when the '36s first came out. Before that I had driven a dilapidated A-model I had bought from a rum-runner down in Galveston. After I bought it I realized that he must have hauled every ounce of bootleg he ever sold in that car. It was on its last legs and as worn out as the sheets in a two-bit whorehouse but Joe Glaviana wasn't the kind of man you return a car to and demand your money back. So I drove the damn thing until I walked outside one morning and found a priest sprinkling holy water on it and administering the last rites. My new car, on the other hand, has an 85 horsepower flathead V-8 and when I gun the engine, it gets up and flies. And I do love to get up and fly.

I turned the car onto Woodhead and went to West Gray where I headed toward downtown. I passed as many cars as I could and was hurtling through the fourth ward like a rocket when an old man in faded overalls wheeled a buckboard loaded with hay and pulled by a pair of mules in front of me. It nearly scared me to death as I stomped on the brakes, blasted him with my horn, and whipped the car around him with inches to spare. He waved at me as I watched him in my rear-view mirror. At least I think he waved — one of his fingers did seem to be unusually long.

I found a parking place behind the Rice Hotel and walked the block to the *Houston Times* building, a freezing wind whipping through the tunnel created by the big buildings. I pushed through one of the four brass-trimmed glass doors, waved at the receptionist behind the big black desk in the center of the rose marble lobby, crossed to the elevator and pushed the big brass button.

The door clanged open with an angry crash. A small dried-up man in a maroon uniform at least three sizes too large for him sat on the stool by the controls. His cap rested on top of his ears and the visor covered his eyebrows. Watery blue eyes glared menacingly out from under the cap.

"Good morning, Bert," I said, deliberately ignoring his churlishness as I had done every work day for the past fifteen years. I noticed something different about him but I couldn't quite put my finger on it. And definitely would not have put my finger on it even if I could have figured it out.

I stepped to the back of the elevator and faced forward, waiting. Nothing happened. He didn't move a muscle. I clenched my teeth, determined not to be the first one to say anything. We stayed there for what seemed like an eternity before he finally asked, "Floor please?"

I could feel my hands opening and shutting and caught myself looking longingly at the back of his scrawny little neck. I had been getting on that elevator at least five mornings a week for fifteen years and every day he asked me what floor I wanted to go to. After I had been working there for about two weeks I had decided to change our routine by jumping on the elevator and chirping "Eight, please" before he could say anything. But when I did that, he snapped that he knew what floor I wanted to go to. Then he muttered about some people thinking just because other people were only elevator operators that that automatically made them stupid.

Once he clanged the door shut and pushed the lever he would begin to tell me some depressing thing that had happened to him at home.

"My wife was cleaning the baffroom last night and accidentally frew my teef down the toilet. They was wrapped in some toilet paper on the sink and she just grabbed 'em and frew 'em in and pulled the chain before she realized it. She offered to call the plumber to come get 'em back for me but I told her

I didn't want the dern things after they'd been in the toilet. Would you?" he asked.

I knew there was something different about him. His mouth was sunk back in his head and he looked like he had swallowed a funnel.

We jerked to a halt at the eighth floor. I realized that he was actually expecting an answer so I mumbled a few words of commiseration and even patted him on the back. I figured that act alone should ensure me a place in heaven. (Not to mention all the other kind things I had done in my lifetime. I didn't really think I'd be running short when I had to account for myself at the Pearly Gates, but it certainly wouldn't hurt to have a few extra good deeds to whip out if necessary.) With these self-righteous thoughts floating around in my head, I stepped out of the elevator.

The entire eighth floor of the *Times* Building was the newsroom. At nine o'clock in the morning a thick haze from cigarettes and nickel cigars already hung over the room like a lonely ghost haunting a graveyard. A group of men was clustered around a desk to my right — guffawing over some obscene joke, no doubt, I thought disgustedly in my pious mood.

"Hey, Hollis!" one of them yelled at me. "Come over here and tell these guys that joke about the traveling salesman you told me yesterday. I can't remember the punchline."

"I can't right now, guys. I've got to go catch Kelly in his office before he heads upstairs to start his daily brownnosing. Why he hasn't died of chronic hepatitis from kissing ass all these years is a mystery to me." I left them guffawing over that one and went to my desk. I was on a roll! I took off my coat, threw it over my typewriter, and headed to the news editor's office.

Out of the corner of my eye I could see Ed McNaspy hunched over his typewriter. He had the mottled face and big red nose of a heavy drinker. He kept a flat chromium flask in his left hip pocket and would pull it out periodically and smack his lips loudly and say he guessed it was time for a little swamp water. Judging by his green teeth, I often wondered if he was serious and really did have swamp water in the damn thing.

I had to pass his desk to get to Kelly's office and I quickened my step hoping he wouldn't notice me. But he lurched unsteadily to his feet and stepped into my path. His pants were too tight and too short. His shirt was grimy and wrinkled and I didn't even want to begin to speculate on the origin of the slimy yellow stuff on his tie. Every time I looked at Ed I could understand Carrie Nation's fanatical need to hack up a bar. I raised my hand in warning and said, "Don't start with me today, Ed."

"Hey, Hollis, how 'bout you and me going out tonight after work? Have a couple pulls on the bottle — go back to your place and have some real fun." He was almost slurring his words as he glanced across the room to make sure the group of men was watching him. They were. The room was so quiet you could have heard the mustache growing on the bearded lady at the carnival.

McNaspy had been pulling this same kind of guff ever since he started working at the *Times* three years earlier. About once a week he'd have recovered enough from the last flailing I had given him to get up the nerve to try again. For some reason known only to him, he actually seemed to think he was going to win one of these skirmishes one day.

"No thanks, McNaspy. I know I'll probably stay up nights regretting my decision, but I think I'll just go home and drink battery acid instead," I said quickly and tried to get around him.

He grabbed my arm and pulled me to him. "What you saving it for, Hollis? It's gonna dry up if you don't use it. Now I think that'd be a real shame, don't you?"

I have a three inch tall bulldyke that lives on my shoulder. She wears a little red tuxedo with sensible shoes, and has a tail and horns. She also carries a pool cue that she jabs me with when she wants me to respond to something I would really rather ignore. She whispers things for me to say and I open my mouth and out they come. My natural instinct was to ignore McNaspy, knowing he wasn't worth the effort. She jabbed, my mouth opened, and I listened with alarm and resignation to what I was saying.

"I'll tell you what's a shame, McNaspy. Some poor woman having to go to bed with you and that tiny little old dick of yours. That's what the real shame is, McNaspy!" I snarled and shoved him backwards so he sat down abruptly in his chair. "And don't you ever lay another finger on me as long as you live, or I'll kick you in the balls so hard, you'll be wearing them for little pink earrings."

As I walked away, I didn't have to look back to know McNaspy's face had turned a darker shade of red. He would spend the rest of the morning stumbling around the newsroom telling everyone within earshot what a "goddamned queer" I was. I didn't particularly like that he did it but then again, I didn't particularly like it that I wasn't born the Queen of England, either. It didn't take too many experiences like that to make you fall down on your knees and thank God you preferred women to men. I hummed "Praise God From Whom All Blessings Flow" as I stomped to Kelly's office.

I banged on the door and then pushed through without waiting for him to tell me to come in. I knew he wouldn't be doing anything anyhow. I was wrong. He was reared back in his chair staring out the window with a blank look on his face. He was a distinguished-looking man in his late fifties and wore tweed coats with leather patches on the elbows and smoked a briar pipe. He looked like he ought to be intelligent but he wasn't. (I had a standing bet with one of the men in the office that if Kelly ever did have an intelligent idea and expressed it verbally, there would be such a vacuum created that his face would be sucked to the back of his head.) He had not been a good writer and he had gotten this job because of his unparalleled skill at bending down to kiss the old wazoo of any superior of his who got within a ten-foot radius. He jumped nervously when I came into the room and reached for a pile of papers to pretend to read.

I went straight to the point. "I want a raise, Kelly. It's been over a year since I've had one. I'm the best crime reporter on this paper and possibly in this town. Last week Richard The Rabbi Goldfein was convicted of first-degree murder almost solely on information I gathered about him. This paper carried that story exclusively. The Associated Press carried a story about me last week that called me a 'brilliant journalist.' " I stopped to catch my breath and to think of some more reasons why I deserved a raise.

"You're right, Hollis. You can have the raise," Kelly said with a beam on his face.

My heart fluttered and I felt confused. I had expected a fight. It couldn't be this easy. I started to ease out of the chair and rush out of the room before he changed his mind. Then I noticed his smile. I've seen more honest faces on men in orange plaid suits lurking around used-car lots. He looked guilty, too. I could feel the skin on my face get tight and the flutter I felt moved from my heart to my stomach. "Okay, Kelly. What's the catch?"

"What are you talking about? There's no catch. You've done a great job and JJ and I both felt you should be rewarded for it," he whined.

It didn't feel right to me. He was as nervous as Confucius in a Santa suit. I thought about putting him through the third degree until he broke under the pressure, but he was already too defensive. I decided to change tactics.

"Sorry, Kelly. I don't know what's wrong with me." I grinned sheepishly. "Be sure and tell JJ thanks for me. Look, I'm going to be running on back to my desk now. I'm fixing to get started working on that story I told you about last week. You know, the guns disappearing from the evidence room at the police station. This is going to be a big one. So I guess I'll go now." I turned to hurry from the room.

"Wait a minute, Hollis. I've got some more good news for you." His smile was beginning to look positively greasy. "You can forget that story. JJ and

I have talked it over and decided to drop it. You're getting a bigger assignment than that one. JJ wants you to cover the centennial celebrations in Dallas and Houston."

I stared at him silently. After a few seconds of this treatment, he began to squirm and turn red. His conscience was about as clean as the floor of a monkey's cage.

"Mr. Delacroix called JJ yesterday and told him to put our best reporter on this thing. He is personally very interested in the centennial. His great great grandfather fought in the Battle of San Jacinto, Hollis. He owns this paper, for God's sake, and he can do whatever he wants to do with it. And he can do whatever he wants to with you, too. If he tells you to stick a light bulb up your ass and blink every time you hear 'The Yellow Rose of Texas,' you will. Do you understand that, Hollis?"

"Now let me get this straight, Kelly," I said calmly. "There are people wearing cement huaraches being dumped every day into Buffalo Bayou with enough bullet holes in them to make a sieve look solid by comparison. The city is being carved into sections by at least five gangsters who would just as soon kill you as look at you. There are marble machines and slots in every cafe, grocery store, ice cream parlor, and pool hall in this city paying off thirty to one if you could ever win, which you can't. The D.A. is screaming for cooperation from the police force, which he is not going to get because the police are too busy driving around in their expensive cars to pick up their payoffs. This city is wide open for every crook, whore, pimp, con man, cokie, bootlegger, and gambler to come in and take his piece of the action and you want me to drop all that and write about a bunch of parties attended by a bunch of people with so much money they don't even have to pick their own noses. Hell, no, they hire two toadies to do it for them — one for each nostril. The highlight of it all will be a bunch of jug-butted men from River Oaks in Houston reenacting the battle of the Alamo with a bunch of equally jug-butted men from Oak Lawn in Dallas while their wives fly off to Paris to spend more money on one dress than most people will earn in a lifetime. Is that right, Kelly? That's what you want me to write about?"

His face had faded from scarlet to white. He looked like I had slapped the color out of him. The phony grin was gone and he was scared. I guess that's what made him such a superior ass-kisser in the first place — his fear of unpleasant confrontations.

"Now, Hollis. There's no sense in getting all upset." His hands flapped like a couple of vultures looking at an armadillo that wasn't quite quick enough to make it across the road. They circled his desk then pounced on his pipe, which he began to fill, nervously spilling tobacco everywhere. He leaned down to blow the tobacco off his desk and accidentally blew off half the papers as well. He looked grateful for the diversion and leaned down to pick them up.

"I will not do it." My voice was cold enough to freeze ice cream. "I will not cover the centennial. I am a crime reporter and I'm good at it." I shut up before I started repeating myself.

"You don't have a choice," he mumbled from under his desk.

"What do you mean I don't have a choice? I have lots of choices. I'd just prefer not to have to use some of them. Get JJ down here, Kelly, and let's settle this thing once and for all."

"Those were JJ's orders, Hollis. He said for you to do it. Period. End of discussion." His voice was becoming shrill.

"Then I quit," I said. My stomach was a knot and my throat felt like it had snapped shut.

His head flew up and rapped the corner of his desk. He bit his tongue at the same time and tears shot from his eyes. For the first time since the conversation had begun, I felt intense satisfaction.

"I can't think right now," he whined pitifully and reached for his handkerchief to wipe the tears that streamed down his face. "You can't quit."

"I just did, Kelly." I whirled on my right foot to leave the room. Big mistake. I pulled something in my right knee, which was already bad from an old injury. Instead of marching out proudly with a dramatic flourish, I gimped out of the room.

I hobbled to my desk, snatched up my coat and gloves then limped to the elevator without looking right or left. I punched the button too hard and jammed my right forefinger. At the rate I was going I'd have to call an ambulance to get home.

The elevator door opened and Bert stared ahead with absolutely no recognition in his eyes. He opened his toothless mouth to ask what floor but before he could utter a word, I grabbed his shoulder with one hand and clamped down like a pair of pliers. I could feel my face grimace from the pain that shot through my jammed finger. Bert's mouth flew open with agony and outrage. He looked up at my face. I narrowed my eyes and my right eyebrow shot up. My lips felt small and hard. His eyes widened and his mouth closed. My hand closed tighter on his shoulder. He kept his eyes on mine. For the first time in fifteen years he closed the door gently and we descended to the first floor in complete silence. I wondered if I had lost the place in heaven that I had gained by being nice to him earlier that morning. I pondered the question for about one tenth of a second before deciding I really didn't give a damn.

I woke up the next morning with a crick in my neck and my whole body as tense as a coiled spring from sleeping while trying to cling to about six inches of bed. That's how I wake up every morning. I go to sleep in the center of the bed with my dog sleeping against my left side. During the course of the night, she shoves and leans until I'm on the edge and the rest of the bed is hers. I don't know how she does it — or why — she only weighs about fifteen pounds. During the winter she allows me a piece of the covers the size of a lady's hankie and during the summer she kicks all of the cover on top of me and somehow pins me under it. I haven't had a decent night's sleep since I got her.

I turned my head slowly and felt her warm breath on my cheek. I could feel her beard, which always smelled mysteriously like hot corn tortillas. I tried to inch her over a little so I would have enough room to lie on my back. Her legs stiffened and her tiny pointed paws dug like spears into my back. I sighed and gave up the fight. My teeth chattered as I rolled out of bed and shuffled into the bathroom.

I turned up the gas in the wall heater, hit the light switch, and accidentally looked into the mirror. I shrieked involuntarily and grabbed the sink for support. When I turned thirty a few years before, I had made a pact with myself not to look at a mirror until I had been awake for at least an hour.

"Oh my God! I look just like Gertrude Stein!" I screamed hysterically. I continued to stare, punishing myself. "That's right, go on and look! Look at that pitiful hulk. Oh, Jesus! My chin is starting to sag! That's something new!"

Just when I was contemplating reaching for the razor to end it all, the phone jangled. I shuffled back into the bedroom and snarled, "Who is it?" although I already knew who it was. The only people in the world who would call me at that hour were Gael and Katherine. I had gone over to their house the night before to tell them about the fiasco at work and we had ended up killing a few bottles of very expensive French wine that Gael kept on hand for special celebrations.

"Hello, Miss Carpenter, this is Mr. Andrew Delacroix's secretary." Gael was using a precise, clipped voice and trying to disguise it by raising it a couple of octaves. Hell, her disguise would have been more effective if she'd just used her normal voice and put on a pair of dark glasses. My eyes narrowed and my mouth tightened into a smirk. I didn't utter a word.

Finally the voice came back on the line. "Miss Carpenter? Mr. Delacroix would like for you to come to his house this evening," she squeaked unconvincingly.

"Ha! You tell Mr. Delacroix that I don't work for him anymore, so when he says 'frog,' I no longer hop. You tell him for me that if he wants to see me, he can crawl on his hands and knees and beg for an audience with me. Then I might lower myself to speak with him. But, then again, I might not. You have a good day now, ya hear!" With a malicious grin I banged the phone down as hard as I could. I could just see the two of them howling around on the floor — what a couple of jokers.

Anice, her eyes little narrow slits, had raised her head from the pillow to frown at me for being too noisy while she was trying to sleep. She yawned to make her point. I grabbed my overcoat, and reached into the bed to scoop her up for her morning walk. She gnawed my finger like a piranha before I could get her up.

"Swell," I said, and hauled her to the front door and tried to snap on her leash. She grabbed it in her teeth and shook it until it was dead and all wrapped around her body and legs. Her eyes cut up from the side to see if I was watching.

"Okay, little wild woman. I see you. Are you finished killing it yet?" I said and untangled her. She gave it a couple more shakes to make sure it was good and dead.

We began our walk, which would take twice as

long since Anice loved to keep me out in bad weather. The wind cut like a knife as we moseyed along. The danger zone was three houses down on the next block. That's where our arch enemy, Mrs. Dantzler, lived. I could see her tiny, red, rat eyes peering out from behind the curtain as we swept by. She didn't allow dogs in her yard (as we had found out after moving into the neighborhood two years ago). She had come shrieking out of her house one morning while I sleepily waited on Anice to be a good girl. She had yelled berserkly at me for what seemed like an eternity. I tried to get her to be quiet, but she would not stop. This morning I waved innocently at the curtain and Anice nodded in that direction. Out of the corner of my eye I saw the curtain drop after we passed into the next yard. Mrs. Dantzler went to sleep every night at 10 o'clock and every night at 10:30 Anice and I made a beeline for her yard for Anice to go to the bathroom. It wasn't something I was particularly proud of but I couldn't seem to bring myself around to stop doing it.

The sky was gray. The wind was cold. The trees were bare. The day was bleak. I liked it. During about half of what we call "winter" in Houston, we have beautiful blue skies and mild temperatures. I wouldn't mind the absence of winter so much if the trees had leaves on them. But there is nothing more depressing than a beautiful springlike day and naked black trees.

When we got back home the phone was ringing and I took my time getting back to the bedroom. I figured it was Gael and Katherine again. They never know when to stop.

"Hello, Miss Carpenter?" a man's voice said. "This is Andrew Delacroix."

I almost ate the telephone.

"Yes?" My voice squeaked like a balloon does when you let the air out while pinching its neck. I tried to clear my throat quietly but it sounded like a train derailment.

"My secretary told me I'd have to crawl to get an audience with you, but I thought I'd try calling you on the phone first," he said politely.

I felt myself blushing and started to explain and then thought to hell with him.

"I was wondering if you could come to the house this evening for drinks with my wife and me?" he asked.

"Today?" I asked, buying time while I tried to think what this was all about. I knew I was a good writer and an asset to the *Times,* but I had not expected the owner himself to call me. I had figured that Kelly would wait two or three days then call me to try to negotiate. Or possibly even J.J. Mattox, the editor-in-chief, would call — but not Andrew Delacroix. I began to feel extremely important.

"Yes, today, please," he said almost apologetically. "I leave town tomorrow for a conference in New York and I was really hoping to talk to you before I left."

"Oh. Uh. Well, I guess today will be okay. I'll need your address, though."

Naturally, where else would he live? I thought as I jotted down the River Oaks address. "All right," I said casually, as though I frequented the houses on River Oaks Boulevard with regularity.

"Good, I'll send the chauffeur to pick you up at a

quarter to five," he said and hung up before I could argue with him.

"I guess he doesn't think peons have cars," I muttered. I went into the kitchen where Anice stood wagging her nub of a tail at me. I prepared our breakfast, which meant I got a new bag of gingersnaps out of the cabinet and a Coca-Cola out of the ice box. We went into the living room, which doubled as a dining room, and sat at the dining table. I put a cookie in front of Anice and took one for myself. I was not that fond of gingersnaps but they were her favorites so that's what we generally had for breakfast.

I took a swig of the Coke and explained about the phone call from Mr. Delacroix. I told her I figured he wanted me to come back to work. She was all for telling him to shove the job up his snobby ass until I told her about needing a job to make money to buy more gingersnaps. She immediately changed her tune and said that life was compromise, negotiation, give and take. Sometimes we had to swallow our foolish pride. I didn't say it out loud but I sure thought she cracked easily under pressure. I just hoped my life never depended on her having to hold up under an interrogation by the enemy. We ate the rest of the cookies in silence. Or at least I ate in silence. She smacked and crunched.

I spent the rest of the day doing chores I never seemed to have time to do and then soaked in a hot tub to get ready to go to the Delacroix home. The hot water felt good and helped my knees, which were really giving me hell in the cold weather. I had ruined them making a fast turn playing dodge ball with a pack of Mexican kids who lived down from my aunt's house in Brownsville when I was eleven years old. My right knee was especially bad. Over the years I had compensated for the knee by putting all my weight on my left leg, which had resulted in a weak left ankle. I hated to think what kind of shape I would be in when I was eighty.

I was dressed and ready when a black Packard eased up to the curb in front of the house at 4:45 sharp. It was so long the hood ornament could have been in Amarillo while the trunk was still in Houston. It was either my ride or one of my neighbors had died.

I walked out of the house and turned to wave at Anice as she sat on her leather ottoman looking out the front window, her gray head tilted to one side. She would wait there sleeping or barking at passers-by until I came home.

The chauffeur got out of the car as I approached and opened the back door for me. He wore a black uniform — to match the car, I guessed. Cute. I stepped into the car ignoring the hand he held out to help me in. He eased the car into gear and we floated down the street like a black thundercloud, the car so ostentatious that I felt like I was riding in a neon movie marquee. I hoped every one of my neighbors saw me — especially Mrs. Dantzler. I bounced up and down on the seat, played with all of the chrome knobs, sniffed the flower in the bud vase, then sniffed the leather seats before I noticed that the chauffeur was watching me in the rearview mirror. We both laughed at the same time. His name was Barry and we were old buddies by the time we turned onto River Oaks Boulevard.

The Delacroix house was three doors down from

the River Oaks Country Club, which was lit up like a Busby Berkeley production. We were on the outskirts of the city. River Oaks formed the western boundary and there was nothing beyond it but woods, bayous, and water moccasins. We turned into a circular drive. The house was a two-story Greek Revival mansion painted white with columns that ran all the way around the house. It was only slightly smaller than Chicago and stood on several acres of some of the most expensive ground in Houston, Texas.

We breezed up the drive through the live oaks and magnolias. The yard was landscaped with azaleas, oleanders, roses, and camellias that would all begin to bloom in about a month. At least the azaleas would bloom in a month. The others would all take their turns after that. The house looked like it could have been plucked out of Natchez or Atlanta and plopped down in Houston, grounds and all. I half expected to see a beautiful woman in a hoop skirt walk out onto the veranda and fall into a swoon.

We pulled up to the front of the house and before I could even get out of the car, the front door was opened by a butler in tails, gloves, and spats. I was beginning to be overwhelmed. The butler's lips moved a sixteenth of an inch at each corner and I realized he was attempting a smile. It looked like it hurt his face. I had a feeling that if he ever accidentally laughed (which, of course, he never would) his face would make a tearing sound like a piece of cheap cotton.

He said, "Follow me, please."

I was glad he didn't say "Walk this way" like a

gag in a Marx brothers movie because I probably wouldn't have been able to keep myself from imitating him walking down the hall. He walked stiffly with the upper half of his body thrust forward and his rear end hiked high up in the air. I tried not to think about corn on the cob.

The floor in the hall was blond wood and for some reason my shoe soles sounded like a couple of sledgehammers banging on railroad spikes as I clumped along behind the butler. I thought about tiptoeing but decided that would be even more conspicuous. I hate it when that happens. Why the hell weren't the butler's shoes making any noise?

He led me into a den that was carpeted, thank God. The entire room was white — walls, furniture, carpet, draperies — even the telephone. An enormous fireplace at one end of the room held a roaring fire. It looked like a set for Jean Harlow.

In a voice that sounded like it came from the grave, the butler told me that Mr. and Mrs. Delacroix would join me momentarily and to please make myself at home. He turned and left the room. What a barrel of laughs he was. I couldn't imagine having him skulking around the house all day. I'd rather stick hot pokers in my eyes and dance on stage in tight shoes and loose panties.

I crossed the room to look at the paintings on the walls. The carpet was so deep I felt like I was wading through the Atchafalaya swamp. The paintings were Monets, Renoirs, Manets and a couple of Van Goghs thrown in for good measure. I wondered if they had the Mona Lisa tucked away upstairs. I was getting numb all over trying to imagine living like this.

I wandered around the room until I came to a set of closed double doors. What the hell. Take a peek. I opened the doors and peered through. It was a war room. There were huge tables with miniature soldiers fighting different battles throughout history. Portraits of famous generals hung on the walls. There were military toys, muskets from the Civil War, swords from the French Revolution, and even an old uniform or two. It was too, too fascinating.

"Andrew's father was a colonel in the army during the great war with Germany," a voice behind me said. "He collected all of that during his lifetime and then left it to Andrew when he died. Andrew is very proud of it."

I turned around to see Lily Delacroix. She was of average height, slender and extremely delicate-looking. Her hair was black and shiny and straight and cut in a sort of long page boy. Her lips were full and red and her skin was pale and smooth. She was the most beautiful woman I had ever seen in my life. She made everyone else in the world look plain and clumpy. But she didn't know it.

I realized that I had been staring at her for a long time. I opened my mouth to say something, but nothing came out. I closed my mouth. I probably looked like a landed carp.

She stood waiting and then she smiled. At that moment someone shot me in the chest with a twelve gauge shotgun. I clutched my chest and staggered backward. I looked down — there was no blood, but my breath was ragged in my throat. At this point I realized that I had not been shot, after all. My chest had simply exploded when she smiled.

"Are you all right?" she asked, concerned. Her

voice was deeper than one might expect and it sounded a little hoarse. I liked it a lot. "You have a funny look on your face.

She crossed the room to me and smiled again, but I was prepared this time. It only felt like a .45 slug. I reeled backwards and sat on the couch. "Would you care for a drink?" she asked.

"Love one," I muttered and nodded.

After she had called for the butler she asked, "Are you sure you are all right?"

"Oh, yes," I reassured her. "I'm fine. I was just up all last night working on a story. I guess I'm more worn out than I realized."

She nodded sympathetically, so I went on making it up as I went, "Sometimes if I get too tired, I have these dizzy spells and pass out. The doctors say there's nothing to really worry about — besides there's absolutely nothing that can be done about it." I smiled bravely.

She nodded again so I kept on talking about my new disease. I could not seem to make myself shut up. As long as she was going to sit there smiling at me, I was going to sit there talking. If I could have gotten her attention by standing on my head dressed in lavender lederhosen and a red babushka, then that's what I would have done. Fortunately, it did not come to that. I was just on the verge of inventing a name for my illness when the butler came in to serve the drinks.

He pulled the cart to the sofa and began mixing martinis in a pitcher. I normally just drink bourbon but decided it might not be the top thing to do so I took a martini and gobbled it down. My mouth had gotten dry from all the talking so I hoisted my glass for a refill. The butler pursed his lips in disapproval. When Mrs. Delacroix turned her head to speak to him, I made a face and stuck out my tongue. He didn't bat an eye.

As I watched her talk to him I felt my heart do the Charleston. She was dressed in a long red gown that matched her lips. I had read many articles on the society page about this woman and her husband. She was called the best-dressed woman in Houston and her clothes were designed by Mainbocher and Molyneux who dressed Mrs. Wallis Simpson. Lily Delacroix made Mrs. Simpson look like a peasant in a $2.98 dress from Palais Royal.

Lily — she had asked me to call her Lily by that time — and her husband were the darlings of Houston's high society. They were rich, beautiful, and well-dressed. I had not expected to like her. I had expected her to be superficial, snobby, and silly. She was none of those things. I would have given anything to be able to touch her.

The butler finally left and we chatted about things in general. We talked about the unusually cold weather, Hitler and Germany, Edward and Mrs. Simpson (whom she referred to as David and Wallis in a totally natural manner not trying to impress me or herself. I found out later that she was a distant cousin of Mrs. Simpson. She was very well-read and knew, or had at least met most of the people who were making the news — including Adolph Hitler. She had met him in Berlin the year before and was afraid of him. She was afraid of how the people had responded to his craziness and told me about having seen an old Jewish man being brutally beaten by a gang of Hitler Youth. She had been on a bus that passed by without even slowing down and none of the other passengers showed any concern. She had begun to scream for the bus to stop and a woman sitting beside her had pulled her back down into the seat and told her to be quiet if she valued her own life. She had left Germany that night and gone to Fort Belvedere, the Gothic folly in Windsor Great Park, to be with the Duke and Mrs. Simpson. She thought that now that the old king had died Edward would marry "Wallis." I disagreed saying that the British would not stand for their king to marry an American divorcee and that he would have to give her up or keep her as a mistress. We were still arguing the point when her husband appeared.

He was tall, slender and dark. His dinner clothes were immaculate and his white double-breasted jacket looked like it had been made by angels. He was handsome in a lizardly sort of way. I had seen him before down at the office but always from a pretty good distance. His lips were too thin and his smile did not reach his black, marble eyes.

The Delacroix were supposed to be the perfect couple. The stories about them in the papers said that they had been in love since childhood. (Their mothers had been best friends.) For some reason or other, Lily had run off and gotten married to an artist in New Orleans when she was in college. The first husband had committed suicide and she and Andrew had finally married about four years ago when she was thirty-five and he a few years older. He had never married and I guess had spent his time pining for her. (I know I would have.) Anyhow, they were happily together as God and their mothers had originally planned.

He smiled liplessly and walked quickly across the room to grasp my hand in both of his. He squeezed like one of those torture boots the ancient Chinese put your foot in to get information out of you. I assumed he didn't realize how strong his grip was until I looked into his eyes and saw that he was very well aware of his strength. I tried to figure out what I had done to make him so angry and then decided the problem was his, not mine. I probably wasn't feminine enough to suit him. I narrowed my eyes, grinned, and squeezed back.

"So, Hollis," he said, still crushing my hand. "I hear there was a little misunderstanding at work yesterday."

"Really? I didn't hear a thing about it," I said, always interested in hearing sensational information of an intimate nature about people I knew.

"I mean between you and Kelly," he said in a tone that implied that he was having to potty train me. I could tell he wanted to say "you blithering boob" at the end of his sentence and was just barely able to control himself. "When you quit your job at the paper," he qualified his statement.

"Oh, that! That was no misunderstanding," I explained airily and waved the very idea away with a very graceful gesture, if I do say so myself. I knocked the long slender brown cigarette out of Lily's hand and had to scramble around on the floor under the white lacquer coffee table praying it didn't burn a hole in the carpet. I recovered it before the hole got too big and figured they could trim the carpet with some small scissors and no one would ever be the wiser. "He wanted me to drop this big story I'm working on about a scandal in the police department and become a society page slop shoveler and I refused to do it. There was no misunderstanding," I said as I handed Lily her cigarette.

"Well, there has got to be a happy solution for everyone here. We've just got to find it. We can't have you quitting the *Times*. Can we, Lily?" he asked his wife and then went on, not really wanting an answer from her, clapping his hands loudly and rubbing the palms together with the gesture of someone who has found the solution for the problem. "I want to hear more about this scandal at the police department. We really can't have this kind of thing happening in Houston. I'm personally very active in the Chamber of Commerce and very concerned with the city's image. I have a certain amount of influence in this town, and believe me, if there is corruption in our police force, I want to know about it. Things will certainly be done to clean it up."

He was as grim and self-righteous as a crusading missionary. He looked at me and I realized that I had been staring at him with my mouth hanging open. I quickly put my finger horizontally under my nose and acted like I had been about to sneeze. I nodded sagely and pursed my lips.

"Well. Tell me about this scandal," he said irritably.

"Oh," I said, stalling for time. "I normally don't discuss the stories I'm working on with anyone. Word may get into the hands of the competition. I also don't want to endanger my sources."

I could tell he was buying it. There really was a scandal at the police department in that a whole warehouseful of guns taken on a raid had disappeared, but a lot of people knew about it. It was not really some big secret that only I knew about. Hell, my source had been the shoe shine boy in front of the courthouse and he'd gotten it from the little newsie pushing the *Chronicle* in front of the Houston Cotton Exchange Building over on Prairie Street. The police department had been so corrupt for so long that it was big news if there wasn't a scandal down there. I wasn't really working on a story about the guns — I just liked to have a story at hand in case somebody asked what I was working on so I could stall them until something came along that grabbed my attention. A kind of smokescreen to keep everyone confused and to make them think I was diligently on the job at all times. People expected me to always be working on some earth-shattering news event, which was simply not possible unless you started making news happen in order to get a story. And I wasn't about to do anything of the kind. If the truth be known, I had decided to give myself a tiny little paid vacation and I wasn't working on a damn thing at the time, but nobody needed to know that.

"Well, I would certainly think you could tell me the story, Hollis. After all, I own the newspaper!" he said in a familiar tone as though we were close friends and I could trust him with anything.

"I'm sorry, Andrew, but I no longer work for your newspaper," I said, using his first name in an attempt to regain some power in this conversation. He was trying to use that old "I'm the strong man, and you're the little lady" tactic on me. It was making me mad. "I'll tell you what. You give me my old job back and forget about this centennial crap and you can read all about this infamy committed by the cops in your very own paper."

"Hollis, Hollis, Hollis." He shook his head and smiled sadly. "I know exactly how you feel. You think reporting crime is the most important job a newspaper has. Wrong! A newspaper reports all news — good and bad. Its purpose is to educate, inform, and entertain the masses. Each one of those functions is just as important as the other. I think this centennial celebration is the biggest news Houston has had in a hundred years! Ha! Ha!" He laughed heartily at his own joke and glanced at his wife and me to see if we appreciated his cleverness. She was smiling sickly and my own lips had pursed so tightly they felt like a draw-string bag.

"I just can't do it, Andrew. It is a physical impossibility for me to write about who designed Miss Edwina Snott's dress that she wore last Thursday night to the very chic party given by Mrs. Rear End in honor of Mr. Peg Leg who is in town visiting his fiancee Miss Jug Butt. I cannot do it. I will not do it," I said emphatically.

"You can't quit the paper, Hollis. The *Times* absolutely would not be the *Times* without you. Why, you are practically a celebrity here in Houston," Lily interrupted, and fired off another round of white teeth and dimples at me. I inhaled so sharply that I nearly sucked the upholstery off the furniture. I could feel myself turning red all over.

Her husband cocked an eyebrow and smiled mockingly at me. I got the distinct feeling that he could read my mind. I could see it in his eyes. I sipped my drink and smiled blandly back at him, trying to make my eyes devoid of all expression.

"Look, Hollis," he said patiently. "This assignment is not what you seem to think it is. I want you to interview some very important people who will be coming here and to Dallas for this event. Hell, I can't just turn any old half-assed hack loose on these dignitaries! The U.S. Congress is voting right now in Washington about allocating money for a monument at the San Jacinto battleground. I need someone with some finesse up there covering that. There's not a soul I would trust to send up there to get the right coverage on that event except you. I need you for this job!"

It was flattering, but it was bullshit. I may be from the big city, but I still recognize a big cow patty when I'm standing on it in the middle of the barn. I couldn't understand what was going on. What did he want from me?

Before I could respond, Lily stepped into the fray. "Look, Andrew. Surely there is someone else who could do this besides Hollis. After all, she is a crime reporter — one of the best in the United States! We're very lucky to have her working for us. I really don't see the necessity for all this commotion."

I turned to smile gratefully at her.

"You stay out of this, Lily." His voice cracked like a bullwhip. "I think I know more about what's going on here than you do. You just sit there and look pretty and leave the thinking to me. I've told you before not to interfere in my business."

Her face froze and turned white with repressed

anger. Her back grew stiff and she sat very straight on the couch as she sipped her drink. Her hand shook slightly as she put her cigarette to her mouth and drew very deeply on it. I couldn't tell if she was scared or angry or both. She didn't say a word.

I had been trying to be more gentle and spiritual recently, so I didn't lean over and jerk his nuts off and grind them into pâté and make him eat it on crackers. His abusive behavior toward his wife pretty much cinched it with me. I wouldn't have worked for the man if he had offered me a million dollars and thrown in Myrna Loy to boot.

I put my glass down on the coffee table and stood up, looking at my watch. "Gee, would you look at that! I had no idea of the time. My how it slips away from you when you are having a pleasant time. I really have got to be going."

Andrew Delacroix crossed to the fireplace and glared at it. His hands had become fists that clenched and unclenched. He snapped his head back and threw the drink down his throat and slammed his glass down on the mantle.

His wife stood up and tried to smile at me with stiff lips. It didn't work. Her shame was palpable. "Andrew, Miss Carpenter is ready to leave now," she said quietly. Her voice cracked slightly.

"Well then call the chauffeur goddammit! Do I have to take care of every goddamn thing that goes on in this house? Can't you for God's sake do anything without having to ask me?"

So much for the perfect couple — the marriage made in heaven.

He whirled and screamed "Jesus!" Picked up his

glass and threw it crashing into the fireplace and stormed from the room. His footsteps rang as he raged down the hall and up the stairs.

"He really is not normally like this, Miss Carpenter. He is under a great deal of pressure lately with all of those trips to New York and Washington," Lily said, covering for the worthless son of a bitch.

I wanted to say something to make her feel better but I just couldn't think of what to say. So I just asked her to have dinner with me some time to tell me more about her impressions about the events that were occurring in Europe.

She smiled shyly and said that she would.

We walked to the front door in silence. She gave me her hand to say goodbye. It was as delicate as a bird's wing. I wanted to say something funny to make her laugh but I merely asked her to call me for dinner some night soon. She nodded again and then the chauffeur was there in the elegantly stylized Packard sedan. I got into the car and turned to wave goodbye to her but the front door had already closed behind her.

Barry wheeled the car down the driveway under trees draped with Spanish moss. At the end of the driveway we had to wait for a break in the traffic pulling into the River Oaks Country Club. From the back seat I watched the Rolls Royces, Cadillacs, Bentleys, and Lincolns sweep by carrying their precious cargo of the powers-that-be of Houston society in their white ties and fur coats on their way to hear the latest in swing bands at their very own club. They would dance the Big Apple and the jitterbug until all hours and think of themselves as daring and exciting.

"Big Valentine dance," Barry announced over his shoulder. It also explained Lily Delacroix's red dress. I had forgotten about Valentine's Day and had not bought Anice any candy. "They have some of the hottest cats in town that play at the country club. I can sit in my apartment over the garage at night and open the window and hear the sweetest swing in town. You like jazz?" he asked.

I nodded, yeah, I liked jazz. Since I seemed to be between jobs at the moment, maybe I could catch a train to New York and go to some places up there like the Cotton Club and the Waldorf Astoria and see some of the big names in person.

Barry blatted the horn until someone finally let us out and we headed back toward Montrose. We passed by the new-style modern shopping center on West Gray with its white bricks and black tiled storefronts. Palm trees lined either side of the street and seemed to have been made by nature to enhance the architectural style. We turned right onto Woodhead by Captain John's seafood restaurant. The pink and green neon sign beckoned people to come into the chrome and glass bar for oysters on the half shell. The outside of the building looked like a boat and was decorated with portholes and big thick ropes and other nautical fittings. I thought about having Barry drop me there so I could swill down a couple dozen raw oysters and a pitcher of beer and forget I didn't have a Valentine — especially one with a red dress and shiny black hair — but I decided to go on home to my dog and listen to the radio for a while.

I told Barry to drop me on the side street by my house so I could check the mail for my upstairs neighbor who was out of town. Besides, this way I could sneak in the back door and surprise Anice. She loved this game.

I went through the back gate and crept through the hall that was an entranceway for both me and my upstairs neighbor. I slithered past the steps that led up to Park's apartment, unlocked my back door, and entered my kitchen.

I tiptoed in and was crossing the kitchen floor heading for the butler's pantry when I realized that something was terribly wrong. The light that I had left on in the living room was off and I could smell cigar smoke. My heart pounded like drums in an African fertility ceremony. I tried to calm myself, to quiet my heart, and breathed slowly through my mouth. I couldn't see in the dark and I closed my eyes to try to adjust them.

In that instant something touched my leg. I had a horror of looking down and seeing some mutilated monster from hell clawing at my leg with a bloody two-fingered hand, but it was just Anice, glad to see me, jumping up and down on her hind legs to get me to pick her up. I snatched her up and put my hand around her muzzle to keep her from talking. As far as I could see, she had not barked once at the intruder but would probably set up a howl at me. She jerked her head back and rattled her tags. It sounded like the noon whistle in my ears. I felt so faint, I thought I was going to just have to lie down and let the angels come take me away.

A voice whispered in my office directly across the hall from me, "What was that noise?"

"I think it was the dog. Don't worry about it. If the dame comes in, you got a rod, aincha? Use it." The voice answering was raspy to the point of being frog-like.

"Let's get outta here, Tully," the first voice said nervously. "This was just supposed to be a simple burglary. Nobody said nothing to me about no killing. Especially a dame."

"Jeez. What a pussy. Okay, you got the thing, we can blow this joint," the second voice rasped like a dull saw being drawn over an oak plank.

I could feel myself sweating with fear. God, just let them leave through the front door. I looked around quickly for some kind of weapon or a place to hide. I felt as helpless as a centipede in a body cast. There was nothing — which I already knew before I even looked. God, just get me out of this one and I promise I'll do something for you. I can't think what it will be just right this moment, but it will be a big one. I glanced longingly toward the back door but was too afraid to move for fear they would hear me. I clutched Anice tightly to me. That damn dog needed to be on a diet, she weighed a ton.

"Let's check around the house — see if there's something we could use," Tully grated.

Electrical charges shot through my body. I didn't know whether to cross the kitchen floor to make a desperate grab for a butcher knife or to just keep still.

Footsteps began to come toward the kitchen.

"Jesus, Tully! I'm about to pee in my pants. We got what we came for — let's get outta here." The first voice was becoming shrill. I hoped they would hurry up and leave — I didn't want burglar pee all over my office carpet.

"All right, goddammit!" Tully snarled.

I heard their footsteps walking away from me toward the living room and then heard the snick of the front door closing. I waited until hell froze over then let out my breath. I finally got my legs to move and went into the hall and back to the bedroom to get my pistol out of the dresser drawer. It was a small Colt .38 and I'd never felt anything so comforting as that revolver. I put Anice down on the floor and began creeping through the house looking through the bathroom, all of the closets, under the bed — any place that someone might hide. After I had assured myself that they were really gone, I locked the front door and turned on a light. My heart was still racing.

I stood in the middle of the living room shaking the gun menacingly in the air at any would-be burglars and snarled, "All right, creeps, come on. I'm ready now."

But, of course, nobody came.

I spent the next two hours going through my desk looking for whatever was missing. I had no idea who had hired those thugs to steal something from my house. I couldn't find anything missing. I looked through all my files to see if they had stolen notes from anything I was working on, but everything was there.

I pushed my chair back from the desk and rubbed my eyes, which were beginning to blur from tiredness. I glanced at the doodads on my desk — books, pens, lamp — everything still in place. I was beginning to get a headache and I laid my head on the desk for a minute. Think! Think! Think! I sat up and rubbed my temples.

I went into the bathroom and took some aspirin, then took Anice for a walk. We sneaked down to

Mrs. Dantzler's to do the evil deed and then rushed back home.

Too tired to think rationally, I got ready for bed. Anice hogged the bed all night even though I explained that I needed more room on nights when I had been severely traumatized by burglars in the house. (It hadn't worked the night before when I had begged for more room on the basis of having lost my job that day, either.)

The next day I felt recovered enough to tackle the problem of why someone had broken in. I took an inventory of the pitifully few facts: (1) They had been after something specific and had gotten it. (2) They had riffled through my files of stories completed and in progress but had not taken anything. (3) There was a possibility they had known I was going to be gone before they broke in. (4) It was also equally possible that they had just watched my house waiting until I left and then had broken in. (5) One of them was named Tully and he croaked like a frog when he talked.

I decided to start with my last clue. (Now I was beginning to sound like a gumshoe in a grade B movie, as if things weren't bad enough already.) I tried to call a friend of mine in the Houston Police Department. Joe Mahan was a sergeant in the records department who I had cultivated as a friend many years ago when I first went to work at the *Times* and he had just been promoted from walking a beat downtown. He was rugged looking and just a shade shorter than average, but he wasn't small. He was gentle to me and not very smart and tended to hold his right hand in his left in a non-threatening manner in front of his chest while he talked to women. He would smile and nod whenever anyone else talked whether he understood what they were saying or not. He wasn't soft, though. He had done his share of handcuffing drunks to fire hydrants and beating the shit out of pimps in back alleys, then yukking it up with the other cops about it over at the Blue Bonnet Cafe on Washington where they all went for coffee. His wife left him and had taken their young son along about the time Joe had begun to laugh at violence. He had never understood why she left. He liked women but whenever he'd had a snootful would tell me that all women dreamed of giving men blow jobs. Somehow it had escaped him in all of his fifty-seven years that the only time that it happened to him was when he hauled himself down to Susie Noble's whorehouse on Caroline and paid for it. Like I said, Joe wasn't too bright.

I called his number off and on all day and never got an answer. He was working a night shift and was usually home during the day. Susie Noble's private number was unlisted and I couldn't find my address book, so I couldn't call to see if he was there.

I caught up on some writing and began an article I figured I could sell to a magazine to bring in some money. I called Gael to tell her about the burglary and she and Katherine asked me to come and stay at their house for a few days, but I declined.

That night I called the police station a couple of times and they said that Joe hadn't come in to work — which he occasionally didn't do, owing to his penchant for whiskey. So I caught up on my sleep and my nerves seemed to be settling back into place.

I started calling Joe early the next morning. I

really needed to talk to him about the burglars. If he didn't know of a criminal named Tully, he had access to records and I was willing to bet that Tully had a record. I knew that for a bottle of good booze, Joe would dig through every record they had until he found the guy or at least someone who could tell me about him.

By mid-morning I decided to drive over to Joe's house to see if he was there and just not answering the phone. I was beginning to get cabin fever and needed to get out of the house. I had been to Joe's once but that had been six years ago and I couldn't remember his address and I still couldn't find my address book. I looked in the telephone directory, got his address, grabbed Anice to take her for the ride, and left the house.

The temperature had climbed to about 65 degrees. We wouldn't have very many more cold days this year. Traffic was terrible downtown and we meandered through the warehouse district on the east side to get to Canal Street. That area was predominantly Mexican but as I turned south I came to the blue-collar neighborhood where Joe lived. I pulled up in front of his house and saw his beat-up gray Chevrolet, which had acquired a few more dents since the last time I had seen it.

An old man was working in his yard across the street painting some old wagon wheels white that he had buried in his yard until only the top half showed. I wondered why he hadn't waited until the weather had gotten a little warmer to do something like that. He watched me suspiciously as I went up the walk to knock on Joe's front door. A raggedy sheer curtain covering the two panes of glass at the top of the door prevented my seeing into the living room.

My shoes got muddy walking through the sparse grass to Joe's back door. He needed to haul in a load of dirt to fill in the low spots in the yard and plant some more grass, but Joe wasn't much on yard work. The yellow paint was peeling off the wooden siding in places, but Joe wasn't much on painting houses, either. I already knew he wasn't much on housekeeping, so I was prepared for that. I banged on the back door, but didn't get a response, so I walked back around and went over to the old man across the street. He watched as I walked toward him.

"Kind of nippy to be out here working in the yard, ain't it?" I asked, dropping into a blue-collar vernacular with a touch of a down-home accent.

His overalls and plaid flannel shirt looked like rats had been gnawing on them. His expression was straight from the dustbowl of Kansas. I'd have been willing to bet anything that he hadn't moved a muscle in his face since Woodrow Wilson was in the White House.

He eyeballed me for a minute with disapproval and suspicion. "You look like that Marlene Dietrich. You from Hollywood?" he asked in a voice that indicated he fully expected me to burst into flames and suffer eternal damnation in the fiery pits of hell.

Yeah, and that's Rin Tin Tin over there in the Schnauzer suit in the car, I thought grumpily. I wasn't flattered. I didn't look a thing like Marlene Dietrich. I knew the old coot was talking about my slacks and saddle oxfords, but I had been wearing them long before Miss Dietrich came to America. Not the same pair of shoes and pants, of course, but the same kind of attire. That's all I ever wore and some old codgers had a problem with it. But I didn't dress to make them happy or to make them unhappy, for that matter. I dressed for myself and that's all I cared about.

I plastered what I hoped looked like a grin on my face and reassured him that I was born and raised in Houston and I even lied that I was originally from this neighborhood and that's how I knew Joe. I grinned at him like we had something in common and he thawed a little bit. An old brown hound dog shuffled out from behind his house and bayed at me like he had treed a coon, and then moseyed over for me to scratch behind his ears, which I did. I could hear Anice barking angrily in the car.

The old man began to look at me with interest. "Jack, he don't usually take to folks like that," he said and although his expression and voice didn't change, I knew he was awestruck.

"You ain't seen Joe around, have you?" I asked, wondering if I was overdoing the accent.

"Naw, I ain't. Not for about two days now. I heard him come in from work yestiddy 'bout three in the morning. Then I thought I heard him leave a few minutes later but I guess I was wrong. I figured he was maybe going out to get his old chicken choked, if you get my meaning," the old man deadpanned it.

I got his meaning, all right. Jesus, that must be all Joe talked about if the whole neighborhood knew about it.

“Maybe I’ll just go on over there and see if he left the door unlocked and leave him a note, then,” I said and told him to have a good day. I recrossed the street and waved at Anice as she stood on her hind legs peering out the car window at me. It would be a while before she forgave me for scratching that hound.

I tried the door and it opened. The house was “empty-house quiet” but I called out his name anyhow. It was even messier than I remembered it. Lord, it was a pig sty and the smell indicated that he hadn’t taken out his garbage for a few days. I headed toward the kitchen to find a napkin to write on.

That’s when I saw him — or at least I saw the soles of his shoes bent uncomfortably and pointed downward as though he were squatting behind the chair hiding from me. I took another step so I could see him, although I really didn’t want to. My stomach was in a knot already and was fluttering up my throat like a bunch of bats heading for the mouth of a cave. He was in a kneeling position beside the dirty overstuffed chair. Blood, bone, and brains were spattered onto the wall, chair, and floor. It looked like somebody had made him keel over and had shot him in the back of the head and he had slumped a little to the left and wedged in the corner made by the chair and the wall.

My breath began to come in big gulps and my nerves were running up and down under my skin like little roller coasters. The hair on the back of my neck was standing up. I was goddamned if I was going to calmly walk over and touch his neck to see if there was a pulse like the hero in movies always did. Hell, anyone could see the man was dead and had been for a good while. I backed out of the house not taking my eyes off the body for fear it would jump up and run at me with its mangled head. I had to force myself not to run, screaming in horror, my brain snapping irretrievably into insanity. I had seen lots of bodies in my line of work, but never one of my friends.

The old man was watching me come back toward him. "You don't look so good," he said. At first I thought he was making a wisecrack about my clothes, but then I realized that my face probably looked like a zombie out of a Boris Karloff movie. "We've got to call the police," I said and my voice sounded hollow in my ears. "Joe's in there dead. Shot in the head."

The old man was probably shocked, but who could tell with that mug of his. We went into his house and he called the cops. His wife came out of the kitchen and brought me some coffee. She made a big fuss over me while we were waiting and even brought me a slice of cherry pie she had made that morning. That was when I vomited on her sofa. It was a hell of a way to pay her back for her hospitality, I know, but there wasn't a whole lot I could do about it at the time.

The rest of the day was pretty much spent answering questions for the police and going back downtown with them to sign a statement. I had found Joe's son's telephone number out in Hollywood. He was working as a waiter at the Trocadero — waiting to be discovered by some big producer who would make him the next Clark Gable. When I got home I tried to call him and was relieved when I didn't get an answer.

I went into the kitchen to fix myself a drink and get Anice a gingersnap. So far, this had just not been my week. I'd lost my job, my house had been burgled, I had found a friend murdered, and I still couldn't find my address book, which was damned inconvenient because I needed to put Tony Mahan's number in it. I sat on my couch for a long time staring at the space heater in the fake fireplace. Anice leaned against me and put her paw on my leg and stared, too.

I got up and went back into the bedroom to check under the bed for my address book, obsessing about it. I tore up the house looking for it, finally gave up, and mixed another drink. I realized that I was focusing on the book to keep from thinking about Joe.

I was so busy concentrating on keeping images of Joe's head out of my thoughts that I didn't hear the footsteps on my front porch. When the knock came I nearly went through the roof. I grabbed my gun, which I had been carrying with me from room to room. I opened the front door and aimed it right at Gael's nose.

"Jesus Christ! What the hell do you think you're doing?" she demanded, eyes wide.

I lowered the gun and stepped back. Gael was my height with shoulder-length wavy brown hair and a strong, square jaw. She walked like a cat stalking its prey, her shoulders squared and every movement controlled and studied. Katherine, taller with blonde hair, looked sophisticated and dressed stylishly. Gael felt the same way about clothes that I did — I had never seen her in anything but pants.

I put the gun on the coffee table and offered them a drink, then told them to go fix it themselves. We finally settled back down in the living room.

Gael owned a construction company. Her face was weatherbeaten from standing outside riding herd over a bunch of lounge-lizard carpenters and painters who were scared half to death of her. Her face was usually as serious as a rattlesnake and her smile was a club she used on unsuspecting women she set out to conquer. She was one of those people who knew everything and insisted on sharing it with others. She had an incredible memory and loved to read about all sorts of subjects and could quote it back to you almost verbatim.

Katherine, on the other hand, was warmer and laughed or yelled a lot, depending on the occasion. She was one of those tall, good-looking east Texas girls.

Gael lay back on the black leather and chrome lounge that was her spot whenever she came to visit. She tidily arranged her cigarettes on the end table, pulled the chrome smoking stand closer to her, found the perfect spot to set her drink, lit a cigarette, and squinted through the cloud of smoke at me.

Katherine sat on the couch so if I said something funny, she could lean over and wallop me, which she did on a regular basis. She asked for the thousandth time when I was going to get a girlfriend and I told her for the thousandth time when I found someone just like her. She smiled and backhanded me. World championship heavyweight boxing matches had probably been won with less punch than was in Katherine's backhand.

Gael grinned watching us. "So tell me why you've taken to greeting your guests at the front door with a pistol up their noses?" she asked, blowing smoke in the direction of the gun on the table.

I told them about finding Joe that morning on top of the other mess that had happened that week, and to top that all off, I had torn up the house trying to find my address book.

Gael puffed her cigarette, which she held between her thumb and forefinger like men hold cigars. She looked wise while she thought about it all. "Maybe the burglars took your address book," she said.

I was stunned. That had never occurred to me.

"Good Lord, I don't think so. What in hell would anyone else possibly want with the thing? There's nothing of importance in it," I pointed out.

"Is anything else missing?" she asked.

"No," I answered.

"Well?" she asked as though her point were proven.

Katherine was petting Anice, who had jumped into her lap and rolled over on her back and was exposing herself shamelessly. "Joe was in your address book and now he's dead," she said casually.

I jumped up in horror. Why hadn't I made that connection? I was supposed to be an investigative reporter and hadn't even seen what was right under my nose. I had just chalked Joe's death up to some old grudge by somebody he had sent up at some time or other. I had considered the timing of his death to be just one more shitty thing that had happened this week. I, who did not believe in coincidence, had let something that obvious slip by me.

Gael was puffed up and pouting because Katherine had figured it out and she had not. She got up to go to the kitchen to mix a drink.

"Why don't you just bring the bottle and ice in here?" Katherine asked, once again pointing out the obvious that had escaped both Gael and me. We both stared at her as if she were the Buddha.

"But why would anyone need to steal my address book to kill Joe? They could have found him by looking in the phone directory," I said, confused.

Gael rolled her eyes heavenward and sighed deeply. "They didn't steal your book to find Joe. They found him in your book and killed him because he was there."

I was getting fuzzy from the bourbon and conversation. "Good grief, you don't think they're going to kill everybody in my address book, do you?" I shrieked.

Katherine reached out to pat my arm and I jumped back, thinking she was going to backhand me. She looked hurt until I explained, then she laughed good-naturedly and popped me affectionately.

"I think whoever took it wanted to know where you get your information from. To find out who your sources are," Gael said.

"So somebody killed Joe, knowing he was a cop, so he couldn't tell me something," I said, finally catching on.

"Something must be going on at the police department," Gael speculated.

"Not necessarily," I said. "It could be any number

of things. I just hope to hell it doesn't have anything to do with those stupid missing guns."

"What guns?" Katherine asked.

I told them about the guns disappearing from the station and how I had mouthed it around so nobody would realize that I actually wasn't working on an assignment.

"That has got to be it," Gael said, rubbing her face with both hands.

"It can't be," I said, and got up to pace. "Too many people knew about it . . . Please, Jesus, don't let me find out Joe was killed because of that goddamned story and my big mouth!"

Katherine said it was time to change the subject because I was just getting more and more upset and nothing could be resolved that night. She was right, of course.

They stayed for a couple more hours trying to convince me to stay at their house until some of this insanity blew over. I refused, but promised to drop by for dinner one night that week and to call them if I heard anything strange.

Anice and I faithfully buzzed Mrs. Dantzler's yard and then I called Tony Mahan and broke the news about his father's death. Before I went to sleep, I prayed for Joe.

The next day I decided to play an ace and go see Bill Oswald. He was one of the most powerful men in the city in an underhanded sort of way and one of the richest, too. He had made a fortune bootlegging during prohibition. Now he owned about one third of the marble and slot machines in operation in the city and ran a floating crap game on the sixth floor of the Lamar Hotel. Most of the richest men in Texas could be found there, sooner or later, including Howard Hughes when he came back to town. I had been in there before when Errol Flynn was rolling dice in the same game as Frank Nitti, The Enforcer from Chicago. There was no telling who you might run into at any given moment at Bill's crap game. Besides the bootlegging and gambling, Bill also ran a herd of high-class whores back and forth between Houston and Dallas. Back in his bootlegging days when he was running booze in from Galveston, he had killed at least two men who were trying to move into his territory. It was rumored that a few others had made the fatal mistake of stepping on his toes, but the bodies had never been located, so nobody could say for sure. His best friend was the sheriff of Harris County and with his man in the sheriff's office and his underworld contacts, Bill knew everything that went on in this city. If he didn't know about it, he could find out about it in a few hours' time — or it simply was not happening.

Joe Mahan had introduced me to Bill years ago. They had grown up together and had remained close friends even after Joe became a cop and Bill took the other side of the law.

Bill lived on South Boulevard in a pink stucco Monterrey-style mansion with a red tile roof. I pulled into his driveway and sat admiring his house wondering if I'd ever have the kind of money it takes to buy one like it.

I got out of my car and went to the door, feeling at least six sets of eyes on me as I walked. His house was crawling with bodyguards. An acorn couldn't fall out of one of the live oak trees that lined the boulevard without those guys knowing about it.

A gorilla in cowboy drag opened the front door before I could ring the bell. I stepped into the living room, which was painted terra cotta with Indian designs stenciled in white. It was furnished in mission oak with Navajo blankets and rugs scattered all over the room. Cacti grew everywhere in pots.

The gorilla left me waiting while he went to see

if Bill had time to talk. He came back quickly and led me to Bill's office.

The office had two overstuffed tan leather chairs across from a desk about the size of the Alamo. A leather couch against the wall matched the chairs. The walls were lined with shelves that held expensive books and Remington bronzes. Three telephones and a dictaphone sat on the desk. There were no windows in the room, and I had always wondered if there was a secret passageway that led out of here.

Bill sat in the big, ornately carved desk chair, and he stood up as I entered the room and came to take my hand in both of his, his mouth stretched in a warm smile. His big dark brown eyes were gentle behind hornrimmed glasses. He was six-feet-three without his cowboy boots, which had a three-inch heel. The boots were made out of extremely rare reptiles, which was fine with me. I'd just as soon all reptiles were made into boots and purses — they gave me the creeps. Bill had thick, crisp, curly gray hair and wore Western-cut suits and bolo ties with silver tips on the ends. The clutch that held his tie together looked like a little slot machine, but I couldn't be sure. He was about sixty years old and looked like a governor or senator — certainly not a mobster.

"Hello, baby." He squeezed me in a bear hug and kissed the tip of my nose. "Where've you been lately? We haven't seen you in a coon's age."

For some reason, Bill thought I was completely and utterly flawless and that everything I said was either terribly important or funny. That made him pretty swell in my book — so what if he'd killed a man or two or three — we've all got to go sometime.

"Rose is going to be upset that she missed you." He hugged me again, then led me to a chair, pushed me in it and sat in the other, turning it to face mine. "She's at the garden club."

Rose was probably the only person in town who didn't know just exactly how Bill made ends meet. She had decided a long time ago that he was a rancher, even though they didn't have a ranch. She went so far as to call his goons "the hands." Needless to say, she had to work hard at ignoring the facts and tended to babble constantly about shallow, meaningless things in order to keep from thinking. She was like a human commode that had to keep flushing to empty her head.

"Did you hear about Joe?" I asked.

"Yeah. I sure hated that." He shook his head sadly. "I loved Joe like a brother. He was a good man. Kinda dumb, though. Spent too much time drinking and getting his monkey spanked down at Susie Noble's place to ever make anything out of himself."

Jesus Christ, I thought. That's all anybody knew about him. They were really going to have to dig deep to find something to put on his tombstone other than "Here Lies Joe Mahan Born June 16, 1878 Died February 15, 1936 He Lived To Get His Chicken Choked." Who in the hell was it that sat around thinking up all these euphemisms?

There was a knock on the door and one of the gorillas wheeled in a table laden with food. Bill had one of the best French chefs in the world working in his kitchen. That's why my visits always coincided with meal time.

"Oh, darn! Is it time for lunch? I thought it was about ten o'clock! Let me get out of here and come back to see you later," I said, jumping to my feet as though to leave.

Bill grinned and pushed me back down into the chair, motioning for the goon to pull the table between us. There was escargot, chicken in champagne, crisp vegetables and croissants with butter and little pots of chocolate for dessert.

"Really, I couldn't possibly eat a thing," I said and patted my stomach. "Anice and I had gingersnaps at seven o'clock this morning. I'm stuffed."

"Eat," he commanded.

I didn't have to be told twice. I snarfed it down quicker than a cannibal could stew a missionary.

Bill ate slowly so I ate his dessert as well as my own. We talked about food and the weather and who had struck oil that week to become the latest Texas millionaire. After we finished eating and Bill had lit a cigar, I came to the meat of the matter and asked him if he had ever heard of a crook named Tully with a gravelly voice.

"That sounds like Tully Kirk to me. Last I heard, he was up in the Panhandle hired for protection by some of those gas strippers. There's been a lot of fighting going on up there with people trying to stop those fellas."

"Well, I guess so. They're only recovering three percent of that gas. Ninety-seven percent is a lot of wastage. I think all sons of bitches that waste natural resources ought to be hung by their thumbs and whipped till they piss on themselves," I pointed out.

"Anyway," he sighed, not wanting me to get on one of my bandwagons, "that's the last I heard of Tully. Why?"

I told him about the burglary and Joe ending up dead a few hours later.

"How come you didn't call the cops after you were robbed?" he asked.

"Well, hell, Bill," I said, astounded. "How can you ask such a silly question? You know as well as I do that if you call the cops to investigate a burglary, nine times out of ten they'll come back and take whatever the burglars left!"

"That's the dern truth," he chuckled. "That Tully you're talking about. He's a tough character. Got his throat cut in a Matamoros whorehouse twenty or thirty years ago and has croaked like a frog ever since. Some people call him the Toad. He's mean and low down."

"You don't know where he might be hanging out here in town, do you?" I asked, knowing he knew everything.

"You might try over at the American Brotherhood Club in the Republic Building . . . in the domino room," he said casually.

He probably could have told me what color tie the man would have on, too. But I figured I could find that out for myself. "Thanks, Bill. I guess I'll mush on over there and see what's going on," I said, rising.

"You sit back down," he said sternly. "Hollis, you know you're practically like a daughter to me and I don't want anything happening to you. I think it'd probably be best if you just forgot about this whole thing."

"Aw, Bill, I know how to take care of myself," I whined. "By the way, did you happen to hear about those guns disappearing from the police department?"

"Yeah, I heard. You know who has them?" he asked.

"Shit, I figured you had them," I laughed. "They keep coming up in conversations and I thought you might know."

"I don't know a thing about them," he protested innocently and held both hands up as if to show me they were empty. "I think they must have been taken out of the country."

"Come on, Bill. You know as well as I do they're stashed in some warehouse either here or in Galveston by some hood. All the senatorial hearings in Washington going on right now, investigating where the mobs get their guns — hell, the police department provides most of them!"

We both laughed as I left. I got in my car and unbuttoned the top button of my pants so I could breathe comfortably after that meal. As I pulled my car around the driveway, I saw Bill's new Cadillac parked outside the garage, gigantic longhorns on the front instead of a hood ornament.

"Jesus H. Christ," I muttered, "what'll he come up with next?"

I drove toward Main Street under the canopy of live oak trees on South Boulevard thinking how scary the trees were with gnarled branches that could take on human aspects at any moment and reach down and grab the car and hurl it into a land of Grimm's dragons and monsters — a land without chocolate and Coca-Cola. I shook off these terrible thoughts and returned to the comforting land of reality — of gangsters, guns, murderers and cheap gin.

The thought of gangsters reminded me to stop at the Crown Jewelry and Pawn Shop on the way to see if I could find a small pistol to hide in my pocket just in case. I had to circle the block twice, fighting the traffic, screaming and cussing the idiots that were out for the sole purpose of snatching the parking place I needed. I almost grabbed my crowbar to jump out and work over an imbecile in a T-model poking along in front of me blowing more smoke than an oil refinery in Baytown, but at that moment I found a parking place and whipped in. I walked the block and a half to the pawn shop and had to take off my coat. It had warmed up to the mid-70s and with the humidity I felt like I'd been transported to the equator. I don't know why we all haven't died of pneumonia with the roller coaster weather in Houston.

Two secretary types were giggling over the three-dollar wedding rings in the window of the jewelry store. I sailed past the rings and bracelets and cufflinks and headed to the case of pistols. Behind the counter a pasty-faced clerk with shiny black hair talked on the phone while eyeballing me with a sneer on his face.

"I'll call you back later," he said, "a customer just walked in." He turned his head and whispered loudly, "She's a . . ." He lowered his voice so I couldn't hear exactly what he thought I was, but I had a pretty good idea. He snorted sarcastically, hung up the phone, and looked me slowly up and down before asking, "What can I do for you, little lady?"

I took a deep breath. "I'd like to look at a small-caliber pistol, please."

He mouthed superciliously about the merits of this one and the capabilities of that one as he pulled them out of the case. His fifteen minutes of officious lecturing were filled with unnecessarily big words, most of which he mispronounced, but then I wasn't there to give him an English lesson.

"Now what in the world would you be needing this gun for, little lady?" He smiled contemptuously.

"I'd be needing it to shoot a man's dick off at twenty paces, so it'd have to be fairly accurate. I'd hate to miss." There she was again, the little bulldyke on my shoulder. I had meant to leave her at home.

The clerk's lips turned as white as a Ku Klux Klan robe as he clamped them together. "Well, I really wouldn't know. We don't have many people coming in here that need a gun for that specific purpose. As a matter of fact, I don't believe I've ever had anyone tell me that's what they needed a gun for."

"Well maybe you didn't bore them as much as you have me. I can tell you right now that if I hadn't wanted to shoot somebody's dick off when I first walked in here, I damn sure would after listening to your officious, condescending crap. Now. I think I'll take that Dreyse .25 caliber vest pocket pistol and a box of cartridges. Please."

His mouth looked like a zipper in a cheap pair of pants and he didn't open it again throughout the rest of the transaction. I had expended more energy on him than he deserved, but I figured if I had saved just one other customer the torture of having to listen to him, then it had been worth it. I sailed out of the store on a cloud of self-satisfaction, knowing that one more time I had done my small part in making the world a better place to live.

I went back to the car, loaded the pistol and stuck it into my pocket. I hoped I wouldn't need it, but after what had happened to Joe, I wasn't taking any chances.

I drove to the Republic Building. The directory showed the American Brotherhood Club was on the seventh floor. I rode the elevator up and touched the gun in my pocket for reassurance.

The bartender, a small wiry man with hair slicked to his head and parted down the middle, stared at me and tilted his head as though he were trying to remember something. "Don't I know you from somewhere?" he asked and pumped his right forefinger up and down to jog his memory. "Yeah, I've seen you somewhere before."

"I don't know."

"I got it," he exclaimed, snapping his fingers and pumping some more. "You work down at the *Times*. Some hotshot reporter or something. My wife knows you. She works at the *Times,* too. I've seen you down there when I dropped her off at work."

"What's your wife's name?" I asked, prepared to lie and say I knew her.

"Ethel. Ethel Fisher. She works in circulation." He beamed.

"I know Ethel," I said relieved at not having to

lie to the nice little man. "She brings me mustard greens from her garden sometimes."

"I grow those mustards out in back of my house," he exclaimed and whipped a glass out and poured me a drink. "On the house. My name's Pete." He stuck out his hand to shake mine while I introduced myself.

I took a sip. With a little imagination, it could very well have been bourbon. I forced myself not to grimace as I sipped it.

"You don't happen to know a Tully Kirk, do you?" I asked casually after I had listened to about all I could handle of stories about his youngest grandchild.

"Wait a sec," Pete said and walked down to the other end of the bar to pour a drink for a customer who had been motioning for one.

I watched the other customers in the bar as I waited for him. A woman with short, blonde, wavy hair sat at a table in the middle of the room sipping through a straw something red in a tall frosted glass. She stared demurely at the table and then quickly glanced at the line of men standing at the bar. A greasy Casanova in a navy pinstripe suit and a tiny mustache eyed her boldly. He gulped down his drink and delicately dabbed his mouth with his napkin. Adjusting his tie he slithered across the room to the woman's table. He said something to her and she motioned for him to have a seat. He leaned over and whispered into her ear and she blushed and giggled. He held up his hand and snapped a finger for a waiter. She looked impressed.

"I hope she's got some money to throw away,"

Pete said as he nodded toward the couple I had been watching. "That son of a bitch comes in two or three times a week to pick up some woman to buy him drinks."

"Damn shame," I said before I asked him again about Tully Kirk.

"Sssht, Tully Kirk," Pete hissed disgustedly and shook his head. "He's a bad one. His favorite weapon's a carpet knife. What you want with him?"

"I just need to ask him a few questions."

Pete rubbed a rag in circular motions on the bar. "He usually comes in around three o'clock to play dominoes. Later he hits some of the dives over on Dowling Street. Likes a little action with one of the girls at Evelina's place, you know? I hear him talk about it."

"You know who his friends are? Where he stays?"

"He was flopping over at the Rio Hotel till a few days ago. Came into some money and moved to the de George. Ain't got any friends, but I seen him talking to Cotton Peeples right before he got that wad of money he was flashing. I don't know what that's all about."

A dern bartender knows everything there is to know about just about anybody that walks into his bar. It never ceases to amaze me. "Cotton Peeples. Isn't he the one that was holding up that Walgreen's and dropped his billfold with his identification in it?"

"Yeah, that's him," Pete laughed. "My wife's always telling me funny stories about old Cotton. He gets caught at everything he does. He stole a car one time and the brakes didn't work — ran into the back of a police car. Dern fool."

"Seems like I remember that," I said. "Have you seen him around anywhere?"

"Sure. Sitting right back there in the poker room. If you want to talk to him, you better hurry. He's been drinking awhile. Liable to pass out any minute now."

I crossed the room and went through the arched doorway and turned left down the hallway, passed the domino room and went to the second doorway on the right into the poker room. I remembered reading about a week before that a man had been killed in this room after an all-night drunk playing cards. I couldn't stop myself from morbidly glancing at the floor to see if there were any big stains. There weren't, thank God.

Nine tables were scattered around the room, which was painted a bright red to keep the players awake. At a small mahogany bar in the corner a bored bartender tried to keep his eyes open. Only one table had players at that time of the day, but the place would be packed in a few hours.

Cotton Peeples was sitting in a corner by himself, nursing a nasty hangover, if I was any judge. I walked over and banged my glass down on his table. He jumped and looked like he was fixing to burst into tears.

"Mind if I sit down?" I shouted while deliberately scraping the chair over the floor with as much noise as possible.

He clutched his head and pressed hard. "Who are you?" he mumbled miserably. His face was gray and doughy. His suit was black and shiny with age. His shirt sleeves and collar were frayed. He gulped down the rest of his drink and looked sadly at the empty glass. He was dead broke. This was going to be easier than I had thought.

"You want another drink?" I roared. The noise intimidated him.

"Sure," he said gratefully. He couldn't make up his mind if I came from heaven or hell.

"You're Cotton Peeples, aren't you?" I asked as I returned from buying a full bottle of whiskey at the bar.

He nodded and I poured him a splash just for being honest.

"You and Tully Kirk broke into my house the other night. How come?" I asked as though I were wondering what time it was.

His head flew up and his mouth flew open. He gaped like a catfish and began to shake his head.

"Come on, Cotton. I don't have all day for this song and dance. I know it was you. Just tell me who hired you and save us both a lot of grief."

He kept shaking his head.

"I'm not going to turn you in to the cops, Cotton, I promise. I just want to know who hired you and why. It'll get you this entire bottle." I pointed to the fifth as though it were Seagram's best instead of something used to remove 200-year-old varnish. The label ought to have had a skull and crossbones on it.

Cotton ogled it like it was ambrosia. "You swear you ain't going to the cops?" He licked his lips, coming about as close to looking like an albino weasel as any human being I had ever clapped eyes on.

"I swear," I said.

"Tully Kirk hired me. We went in to look for

some papers and an address book," he whined. "That's all I know."

"Now, Cotton. You and I both know Tully Kirk hasn't got any reason for wanting my address book. Somebody hired him and I want to know who that was."

"I don't know nothing about that, honest to God. You'll have to talk to Tully about that," he said as his eyes rolled around his head with fear and rot gut.

"What did you do with my address book?"

"Tully took it with him. Me and him split up after we left your house and I ain't seen him since."

"Why do I have this sneaking suspicion you're lying to me, Cotton? I don't think you're going to answer the 500-dollar question and win the booze," I said sadistically.

"Please. I ain't lying. I really could use that whiskey."

I almost felt sorry for him but then I remembered how scared I'd been standing in my kitchen listening to them talking about killing me. Then I thought about how they could have left the door open and let Anice out to get lost or run over. I leaned over and placed a saddle oxford on top of his shoe and ground down with all of my weight — and I'm not skinny by any definition of the word. His face paled even worse than normal.

"I ought to beat your tiny little brains out but I haven't got the time it would take to find them so I could beat them out — which is your good fortune. That makes this your lucky day, Cotton." I whispered, since the bartender had begun to watch us suspiciously. "I'm going to go find Tully and if I find out you've lied to me, I'm going to come back and hang you up by your hair until every time you blink your eyes, your goddamn britches legs roll up like window shades." I didn't normally rage around town threatening to shoot and beat people, but these were unusual times and it seemed to be working.

I ground my foot into his toes again until I heard a satisfying pop, then left the poker room and went back out front to talk to Pete.

I noticed that Don Juan had finagled the blonde into a booth against the wall and was drawing the curtain for privacy. It was a good thing he had two hands — one to dig in her purse while the other pawed her.

Pete said that Tully hadn't shown yet, so I ordered a cup of coffee and took it to a table to gather my thoughts. I really hadn't thought out what I was going to say to the Toad when I caught up with him.

I sat and watched the activity in the bar for a while. There were quite a few more people in the place than when I had first arrived. The men stood at the bar in their suits and hats eating peanuts and drinking while the women sat at the tables, just drinking. I wondered if it was considered unladylike to eat peanuts in public as I munched a handful. If that was the case, I'd have to start throwing them up in the air and catching them in my mouth from now on. I waited until about four o'clock, drinking coffee but the Toad never showed. There were groans and thumps coming from behind the curtain in the booth occupied by the blonde and Romeo. I wondered how far they would go, but decided I didn't have the time to stay and find out.

I went over to the phone on the wall near the entranceway and called the de George Hotel to see if Tully was registered there. The clerk said Mr. Kirk was in his room and did I want to leave a message. I told him no and hung up.

I drove over to Preston and parked in the hotel parking garage. The parking attendant nodded at me as I headed for the double glass doors that led to the lobby. I walked over to where he sat on his stool. He jumped up, "Yes, ma'am."

"Hi. I was wondering if Tully Kirk was back yet. I was supposed to meet him here and I'm a little late. If he's already here, I'll just run up to his room, if you know the number," I said hurriedly and sincerely.

The attendant looked at me without blinking. He put his hands in his powder blue uniform pockets and stared at me as though I had suddenly lapsed into Hindustani. I sighed and pulled out a dollar bill.

He grinned and his hand snatched the dollar and disappeared as quickly as an anteater's tongue. "Room 504," he said owlishly.

I went into the lobby and over to the elevator. I wandered down the hall to 504 for a minute, wondering what to do. I finally sucked in my breath and knocked on the door. Nothing. I knocked again and thought I heard a noise but no one answered the door. I breathed quietly through my mouth as I tried the doorknob. It wasn't locked. My heart banged deafeningly as I slowly opened the door. I was going to have a heart attack if things didn't lighten up. I half expected a gunblast as I stepped into the room. I took a step forward and froze.

A man who I assumed was Tully Kirk sat in the chair by the bed looking at me. His face was so bloody I couldn't tell what he looked like. Blood had soaked his pink shirt and run down onto his mustard-colored pants. I don't know if I winced from the bloody mess or the color combination. I started backing out of the room when he groaned. I realized he was not dead.

I went reluctantly over to where he sat and stared at him. "Goodness gracious sakes alive. I don't know if you're aware of it, but somebody has beaten the holy shit out of you," I told him.

His one good eye rolled up into his head. I went into the bathroom and picked up a towel and wet it in the sink. A half pint of Jack Daniels sat on the back of the lavatory, so I picked that up, too. I went back into the bedroom and handed him the towel. He took it in his left hand since his right one had been broken finger by finger until it looked like a catcher's mitt. He wasn't going to be much danger as a hired gun ever again unless he was really good with his left hand and I doubted if he was. Most people couldn't even eat peas with a fork using their left hands, much less be an accurate shot with a gun.

I drank most of the whiskey while he wiped his face, then I passed the last swallow to him. I took the towel and rinsed it out while he drank. He wiped his face some more. One of his eyes was swollen completely shut, his nose looked like a pancake, and his lips looked like a couple of inner tubes.

"You want me to get the front desk clerk to call a doctor?" I asked.

He shook his head slowly and groaned from the pain of doing it. "Whiskey," he mumbled.

"We drank it all. I needed it to calm my nerves after looking at your face," I said without the least bit of guilt.

"Suitcase," he muttered.

"You don't need to be going anywhere," I said.

"Suitcase," he muttered pushily.

"Oh, you want me to look in the suitcase," I said, catching on.

I went over to the brown suitcase lying on the floor at the foot of the bed. In it were a couple of shirts and some underwear and an orange tie with a hula girl in a grass skirt painted on it. Jesus Christ! It was remotely possible that someone had beaten the shit out of him for his poor taste in clothes. Under the shirts I found a brand new bottle of whiskey. I quickly opened it and took a pull. I heard a groan and saw that the Toad was reaching out his left hand, gesturing for the bottle in a beseeching manner. I handed it to him and even helped him get it to his lips. He drank for a long time and I finally took it away before he got to where he couldn't answer my questions. He looked at me with a question in his eye.

"Who?" he asked.

"I'm Hollis Carpenter. You broke into my house the other night. Remember?"

He blinked his eye and nodded. I was surprised that he admitted it.

"Who hired you?"

"Cotton," he muttered.

"Yes, I know Cotton was involved. I want to know who hired you."

He shook his head slowly and grimaced — at least that's what I think he did.

"Your hand hurting enough for me to call the doctor yet? They could put you in the hospital and give you a shot of morphine. You wouldn't feel a thing."

He nodded. "Call."

"As soon as you tell me who hired you, you asshole," I said, not giving a damn how much pain he was in.

"Cotton," he said emphatically.

"Come on, Tully. Cotton doesn't know anything. He's just a pitiful old drunk."

"Lies. Cotton hired me." He gritted his teeth.

"I'd hate to have to shake your hand," I warned.

"No. It's true!" He looked at me fearfully.

I was getting tired of hanging around the dump. I leaned over and wiggled his pinkie. He screamed from the pain. "I swear!"

"Okay, okay," I said, letting go of his finger.

"Drink," he begged.

"Don't mind if I do," I said and polished off the rest of the bottle. "I'll go call an ambulance now."

"Drink," he said again.

"Oh, you wanted a drink. Sorry. There's none left," I said without remorse.

He seemed relieved to see me go. I went downstairs and told the desk clerk what had happened and waited as he called St. Joseph Infirmary. After that was done, I left the lobby and went to get my car.

The attendant was still sitting on his stool. I crossed to him again. "I'll bet I wasn't the first person today to ask you for Mr. Kirk's room number, was I?"

He stared blankly at me. I pulled out another dollar.

"Cowboy dude," he said as the money whiffed through the air as silently as a Rolls Royce leaving the showroom and did the, by now, familiar disappearing act.

I went on to my car. Cowboy dude? Cowboy dude. That didn't narrow things down much considering we were in the middle of cowboy country here in Texas. I went back to the Republic Building to look for Cotton, but Pete said that he had left right after I had. I went home to walk Anice.

I lay down to close my eyes and think about the events of the day. Things seemed to be getting more and more confusing and out of control. I felt like the only thing I had done all day was to eat and drink too much and run around flailing my arms. My brain was spinning and swirling off into space and I couldn't seem to get centered enough to see what was happening. I lay perfectly still and concentrated on a spot in the middle of my forehead to meditate like a Buddhist monk so the answer would come. I was just beginning to feel in control of myself when Anice jumped on my stomach. The only thing apparent to me at that moment was that Buddhist monks probably didn't let dogs have the run of the temple.

I shoved her off before she ruptured something, and I closed my eyes again. The most curious thing

I could think of was that it looked as though Cotton Peeples had hired Tully and not the other way around. With as much pain as he'd been in, I believed that Tully was probably telling the truth. But who on God's green earth would hire Cotton to burgle a place and possibly kill someone? And who beat up Tully? And why?

I gave up and dozed off for a couple of hours until the telephone woke me up. I grabbed my temples to stop the dull ache and clutched the earpiece of the phone.

"Hello?" I croaked just like Tully. My eyes felt like sandpaper and I couldn't seem to get any oxygen into my system. I vowed at that moment not to touch another drink for at least a month and maybe for the rest of my life, no matter what.

"Is this Hollis?" a hoarse feminine voice asked.

"Yes," I answered. My brain was idling in neutral and would not shift into first.

"This is Lily Delacroix. We met the other night. You had said something about getting together some time and I wondered if the offer still stood?"

I grabbed the mouthpiece of the phone and cleared my throat enough to say yes.

"I was thinking we could meet for a drink tonight."

"Tonight?"

"Yes, if you can."

"Oh, sure. I was just thinking about how much I'd love a drink about right now."

"Wonderful!" she said and seemed to mean it. "Do you have any special place you'd like to go?"

"You pick a place and I'll be there," I said, unable to think of a place that didn't have so much spit on the floor that she'd slip down in her high heels.

"All right. How about the Hunt Room at the Warwick?"

"Sure. It's going to take me at least an hour to get ready and get there, if that's okay."

"That's fine," she said. "See you there in an hour."

I calmly hung up the phone and walked sedately into the bathroom and turned on the faucets to run a hot bath, Anice prancing behind me. I took two aspirin and went back into the bedroom to carefully peruse the contents of my closet. I controlled myself in this sophisticated manner for another three seconds before I jumped in the air and screamed "Yeeeha!" and scared Anice half to death.

Having this incredibly beautiful woman call me up to meet her for a drink was no more implausible than anything else that had happened so far that week. I knew she just wanted to try to persuade me to come back to work, but the prospect of sitting and looking at her for a couple of hours was pretty thrilling. It sure beat the hell out of running around town looking at nasty old crooks in mustard-colored pants. I was feeling more and more like Alice In Wonderland as more and more things took on an unrealistic aspect. Oh, well. I decided that the only thing I could do at this point was to jump in and start swimming since thinking hadn't gotten me anywhere so far.

I was as nervous as a flea on a hophead and couldn't decide what to wear so I went to the front door and stuck my hand out to see what the temperature was. It had gotten cold again. Swell. I went back to the closet and dragged out a pair of brown wool pants and a cream-colored sweater. I soaked in the tub until my joints quit aching and I began to relax for the first time all day. Then I thought about Lily again and screamed involuntarily. There was no way I could remain cool and calm in those circumstances. Anice hid behind the commode thinking I had taken leave of my senses, which I had, until I picked her up and squeezed her and told her how much I loved her. She wiggled and looked relieved, then pranced when I put her down.

I threw my clothes on and stuck my good luck diamond stud in my left ear. My saddle oxfords needed polishing, but I didn't have time. I splashed on some perfume and grabbed my coat and keys. Anice reared at the front door, waiting to go with me. I told her she had to stay at home, but I wasn't strong enough to withstand the look on her face so I grabbed her up to go with me. She would rather ride with me and wait in the car than stay home by herself.

We rolled out onto Woodhead and headed south. My mouth was as dry as a temperance hall and my heart raced in a good way. Anice immediately got in my lap and stood on her hind feet pawing at the window so I would roll it down. I tried to tell her it was too cold — especially since my hair was still wet — but she insisted, so down it went. She hung way out with her beard and eyebrows blowing backwards and her hind feet digging like screwdrivers into my leg.

We whipped a left onto Richmond. I was nervous and couldn't imagine why Lily had called me, but I really didn't care at that point. I was attracted to her. I didn't want to be, considering the circumstances. A married heterosexual woman is not exactly my idea of a good prospect. I usually never even looked twice at them, but there was something about this woman that made me ignore the warning bells.

I turned right onto Montrose Boulevard and had to grab Anice's hind legs to keep her from pitching out of the car onto her hard little head. I cussed, turned the wheel, shifted down, and hung on to Anice all at the same time. She barked excitedly and tried to hang even further out. We passed the museum in grand style and breezed magnificently into the Warwick drive. A valet opened the car door for me as I rolled to a stop. He got in the car and I smirked evilly as I heard him scream when Anice jumped into his lap and stomped his testicles to get to the window to stick her head out.

The doorman looked like a Russian czar in his uniform and was almost intimidatingly dignified. I would have curtsied if I'd known how. I tried not to walk like I was measuring cotton fields as I sailed into the hotel lobby — my small concession to femininity.

The lobby of the Warwick was lit by a crystal chandelier the size of a small ship. The panelled walls were a light walnut, and an Aubusson tapestry covered the wall opposite the front door. A rug the color of coffee with cream covered the off-white marble floor. The things that were supposed to sparkle and glitter did, and the things that were supposed to be dull and flat were. There were six small shops on each side of the lobby selling clothing, gifts, and jewelry. I walked past the front desk and down a hall to a palm court where people sat smiling and talking to each other, drinking coffee and eating French pastries.

A door across the court had a sign over it that said Hunt Room. I walked past the huge palms in their big brass pots and looked in. The room was very dark with varnished wood paneling. The chandeliers were made of huge brass hunting horns. A gas log fire burned in a fireplace of brown marble. It was my favorite kind of place to have a drink — dark, romantic, and not a single peanut hull on the floor.

My eyes finally adjusted to the darkness and I saw Lily sitting at a table in the corner. She smiled and my knees buckled; I almost pitched into a heap on the floor. But I drew a deep breath and crossed the room. She watched me as I walked toward her. I wished she would look away in case I tripped over something — gracefulness not being one of the traits I'm best known for. I managed to make it to the table without making a fool of myself. I would have been less afraid of fighting the Battle of Gettysburg wearing a pink satin tutu and armed with a baton than I was of sitting down and carrying on a conversation with that woman. I kept having to remind myself that she was just an ordinary human being but I knew I was lying. She was a goddess straight from Olympus and I knew it.

A waiter magically appeared, grinning like the Cheshire Cat, took my order and left. I half expected his grin to remain some time after the rest of him had gone.

I prayed fervently for the waiter to hurry back

with my drink because I had just realized that my mouth was so dry I couldn't speak. I smiled and nodded.

"Hello. How are you?" she asked as she picked up a red cigarette with a gold tip and lit it with a gold lighter. The lighter went snick as the lid opened and snick again as it closed, unlike the clang of cheap Zippos that mere mortals used. Her cigarettes had probably cost more than my sweater.

She wore a black dress that matched her hair and eyes. It made her look French for some reason and I told her so. She laughed and said that her ancestors had been French. They had just barely gotten out of France one step ahead of the guillotine and had eventually ended up in Louisiana. My own family had waded out of the Irish bogs to get here. (Probably grunting and shoving and slapping each other the entire trip over.) She told me amusing anecdotes about her family and I began to relax, aided by the fact that the waiter appeared and reappeared with fresh drinks before I could finish the last sip of my old one. Elbows on the table, I propped my chin in my hands, staring at her as she talked.

She finished a story and looked at me expectantly as though it were my turn. I kept staring. She reached up and flicked her hair away from the back of her neck and then shook her head so that it shimmered and fell into place. I couldn't have been more fascinated if I had watched Shakespeare himself performing Hamlet buck naked.

My left hand rested on my hip and my chin still rested in my right hand. "You are beautiful." I stated the fact. I was not flirting. It was just a fact like the sun would rise tomorrow — there was simply no getting around it.

She blushed shyly. "You aren't so bad yourself," she said and ducked her head. She looked at me and sipped her Courvoisier. "Can I ask you a personal question?"

Oh, shit, here it comes, I thought as I nodded. I might as well get it over with.

"Do you like women?" She nervously picked up another cigarette and lit it.

Yes was all I said. What else can you say? This was where most heterosexual women ran squealing from the table.

"Good. I'm glad." She said it simply as though it were the normal response.

I had been wrong — she was light years beyond being a goddess. There was not a word to describe her. My heart fluttered like a hummingbird with his beak stuck in honeysuckle and my face felt prickly and hot.

"Why did you call me?" I asked finally.

"I don't know. I just somehow felt that you were someone I could talk to. Something is happening to me that I don't understand and there is no one that I feel that I can confide in."

"What about your husband?" I had to ask. I wanted to go ahead and cut to the heart of it. I wanted to hear it from her that she couldn't stand the son of a bitch.

She shook her head and her eyes glistened with tears. She dashed them away with the back of her hand and I handed her a cocktail napkin. "Would you excuse me while I go to the ladies room?"

I shook my head and then realized that I needed to be nodding instead. So I nodded instead. She stood up and walked away from the table. I don't know what I had expected when I had come over here to meet her but I don't think it was this.

She came back and told me that she had never really loved Andrew. She had run away to New Orleans with a boy who was her best friend in college and married him to get away from Andrew. It turned out that the boy was homosexual and had been beaten to death one night, his body dumped in Pirate's Alley near the apartment he and Lily shared. The police told her he'd probably been killed by someone he had picked up at one of the bars on Bourbon Street. Her mother had never stopped wanting her to marry Andrew and had told her over and over how perfectly suited they were until she kidded herself into believing it and married him to please the old bat. (My description of her mother, not hers.) She was sure that he was just as unhappy as she was with their marriage but was too polite to say so.

"I should never have gotten married. I am frigid. I've known it all my life," she said, ashamed and angry at herself.

I handed her another napkin to cry into. I glanced wild-eyed for the waiter. I was in desperate need of another drink. I flailed my arms for him to hurry.

"I should not be telling you this. But everyone thinks we have a perfect marriage and there is not another soul I can talk to. I don't know which way to turn."

"Where is Andrew?"

"In New York. He spends three weeks out of the month there. He says it's business but I know it's another woman. And, God help me, I'm glad. You don't know what a relief it is not to have some man coming at you in bed and wanting to scream in horror while he is having sex with you."

I may not know, but I could imagine, and that was enough for me. I gulped my drink and searched for something appropriate to say. "You can't live your life for other people. What is the absolute worst that can happen if you divorce him?"

"I think it would kill my mother."

"No, it won't. She may try to make you think it will, but it won't. And if it does, so much the better as far as I'm concerned. I can't stand a woman who manipulates her children into doing things they don't want to do. She was strong enough to make you marry him. Believe me, she'll be strong enough to live through the divorce."

"I'm so ashamed," she said miserably. "I feel like such a failure. I feel like I have failed my mother one more time."

"The only person you've failed is yourself. What would you have done if you had not gotten married? What did you want to be when you were growing up?"

"I wanted to be an artist," she said, sniffling into the napkin.

Thank God. I grasped at the subject like a life jacket on the Titanic. We talked about art, which she had majored in in college. She had also wanted to be a jeweler. I encouraged her to take it up again and as she talked she began to glow. She became enthusiastic and excited at the idea and said she would buy some equipment and take up her old art.

A woman had begun to play the piano by the bar and was crooning songs in a voice that was pure, raw sex. We talked for a long time and listened to the singer. Lily was happier than I had seen her before, probably from having talked about the secret she had carried around inside her for so long — as though the world had been lifted from her shoulders just by telling someone else that she was unhappily married. It was incredible how much happier people were when they quit pretending and lying and hiding.

"I need to go call my chauffeur to come pick me up," she finally said, glancing at her watch. "I'm on a committee for some of the centennial celebrations and we're having a meeting at ten in the morning."

I looked at my watch, surprised to see that it was one o'clock in the morning and that we had been talking for almost three hours.

"Let me give you a ride home," I offered. It wouldn't be that much out of the way and I wanted to prolong the evening.

"Are you sure it's no problem?" she asked.

The valet pulled the car around. Anice piled into Lily's lap as though they were old friends and I drove toward River Oaks. We talked comfortably together and I deliberately took a long way around but finally ended up at her front door.

"Thank you for the ride and for listening to me," she said. "I'm afraid I burdened you with my problems, but I promise I won't mention them again next time."

I reassured her that it had been no burden and told her she could talk to me anytime she needed to.

She reached for the door handle, hesitated, then leaned toward me and put her arms around me and hugged me. "Thank you, so much."

I hugged her back. Her head moved against my face. She turned to face me to say something else and when she did, I kissed her on the lips. I don't know what possessed me to do it — it just seemed like the thing to do at the time. I could have kicked myself for doing it after the way she had trusted me. She sat stock still and I expected her to jerk away and jump out of the car. Instead, she put her arms around my neck and pressed her lips to mine. She opened her mouth and when my tongue touched hers, I felt electrical shocks running up and down the front of my body from my pelvis to my heart.

She pulled away from me and gasped. "This is wonderful," she said, and looked at me with wide eyes. So I kissed her some more. I shook like a leaf and my legs felt like water.

"This is just great," she said, laughing and crying at the same time. "I've never felt like this before. What is happening?" She was completely naive and childlike and my heart felt as though it would break. My right hand was on her knee. She took it and placed it between her legs and said, "Lightning is striking me here and running through my body and exploding out the top of my head. What is happening?"

"As it turns out, you're not frigid," I said, trying to get a grip on myself so I wouldn't go shooting through the roof of the car like a rocket. She laid a hand on my cheek and kissed me again.

"Come spend the night with me," I rasped, sounding like I had strep throat.

"I can't. I have got to go to that meeting in the morning. Can I see you tomorrow? I would like to do this some more!"

"You bet." I laughed at the formal way she expressed herself. I liked everything about her. Anice sat on the floor of the car watching in disgust because she had not been able to wedge herself in between us.

"I've got to go in to bed. Will you call me tomorrow?"

"I've got a lot to do tomorrow,' I said. "Why don't we just plan on doing something tomorrow night and I'll call you as soon as I can in the evening."

"All right," she said dreamily and kissed me again. She got out of the car and I waited until she got to the front door and had it open before I cranked the car. The windows had fogged up and I laughed as I wiped them off with a towel that I kept under the seat for emergencies.

I waved at her as I drove off and I could see her out of my rearview mirror standing in the doorway watching until I turned out of her driveway.

At least one mystery had been solved. There was no longer any doubt in my mind why she had called me to go and have a drink, although she had probably not been aware of it consciously when she had made that call. I sang all the way home and didn't even honk at the asshole who cut in front of me as he pulled out of the River Oaks Theatre.

When we got home, Anice and I walked around the outside of the house, peering in windows and listening for voices. I didn't want to walk in on any more surprises. Feeling like a dime store detective, I searched the house, pistol in hand, before relaxing on the bed and thinking of Lily Delacroix.

I didn't like it that she was married and had never been with another woman. Little voices in my head were screaming to stay away from her. There wasn't a solution to this thing without someone getting hurt. And I damned sure didn't want it to be me. I shook off the thoughts that come late at night like spooks from the grave rattling their chains and moaning in pain. Knowing things wouldn't seem so hopeless after a night's rest, I closed my eyes to sleep.

The phone woke me up. I couldn't believe it.

Three o'clock in the morning and my goddamn phone was ringing. I groped for it blindly. A man's voice grated hoarsely, "I'm going to kill you. You can run and you can hide, but I'll find you and kill you."

I shot up in the bed and stared at the phone. He was still on the other end — there wasn't a dial tone. I waited, hoping it was a joke. He muttered obscenities that would have shocked the madam of a Singapore brothel. I slammed the earpiece down. My hands were shaking. The man had obviously disguised his voice to make himself sound demented. Maybe he didn't realize those words were demented enough without disguising his voice. I didn't know who it was, but it sure as shit wasn't the neighborhood welcome wagon catching up on a backlog of calls.

I wanted a cigarette but I couldn't have one — it made my dog sneeze.

I sat on the edge of the bed trying to think who would want to kill little ole me. The list was so long that I had to narrow it down to the last six months. I could think of at least seven politicians, five gangsters, two city officials, and a partridge in a pear tree. Anice glared at me through beady eyes, letting me know she didn't appreciate my turning the lamp on in the middle of the night. I ignored her and went to the dresser to get the .38 out of the drawer. I checked the chambers and slid it under my pillow. I turned out the light and thrashed until I finally went to sleep.

I dreamed that Lily took me home to meet her parents. They were sitting in bed fully clothed under the covers, so I got in bed with them and began to talk. A small bird came into the room. It was about the size of my thumb and was a bright red color, with two heads, and feathers on its back that looked like two great big eyes. It represented love and harmony. I chased it all night long.

The telephone woke me up again at a little after seven. I snatched it up and snarled hello into it.

"Good morning," Lily said.

"Hello. I thought you were going to be someone else," I explained. "I mean on the phone. I got an obscene phone call last night and I thought he might be calling back."

"Oh. I'm sorry if I woke you up but I wanted to catch you before you got going this morning."

My heart sank. She had changed her mind. She was calling to make an excuse for tonight and I would never hear from her again.

"I just wanted to tell you that Benny Goodman is at the Rice Terrace tonight and I wondered if you'd like to go hear him?"

"I would love to. I've tried to see him every time he's been to Houston and something has always come up to prevent it. What time?" She could have asked me to go hear a concerto of people scraping their nails on a blackboard and I would have said yes.

"Nine o'clock."

"Okay. Do you want me to come get you or do you want to meet there or what?"

"Why don't I just meet you there? Out front at eight-thirty."

"I'll be looking forward to it all day," I said.

"So will I."

"Oh, uh, Lily. When did you say Andrew would be coming back to town?" I asked casually.

"I don't know. Probably in about two weeks. Why?"

"No reason. Just wondering."

"Oh. Well, have a wonderful day and I'll be thinking about you."

"I'll be thinking about you, too." Ha! I probably wouldn't think about anything else for the rest of my life.

"I've got to jump in the shower now, but I'll see you tonight," she said and hung up.

I lay back on the pillows and envisioned her in the shower. I knew just exactly what she would look like. I wasn't going to get much done today if I kept thinking about that. I wondered if she would end all of our conversations with statements like I've got to go to bed or I've got to jump in the shower. I hoped not. My imagination was too active as it was, and given even the slightest encouragement could get totally out of hand. I had a lot to do so I rolled on out of bed instead of lying there with my eyes glazed as though I had a brain concussion.

After walking Anice I jumped into my own shower. The warm water pounded my head and cleared away a few cobwebs. I tried to get my ducks in a row for the day. I naturally needed to find Cotton Peeples but that would take time I didn't have to spare. I needed to go by Susie Noble's house-of-ill-repute and see if Joe had been there the night he got killed. Besides, it had been a long time since I had seen Susie and I was crazy about her.

The first thing I needed to do, though, was to find out about Joe's funeral. His son had said that he would fly in either that day or the next and had asked if I could pick him up at the airport. He had also said he would make the arrangements by phone with Earthman's Funeral Home for the day after tomorrow.

I called the Houston Police Department and asked for homicide. The captain of that division was Frank Brumfield, a handsome, easy-going man in his early sixties. We were tight. Over the years, I had been able to give him some information on several investigations and he had given me a couple of exclusives.

Unfortunately, Frank was not in and Sergeant Darryl Wade answered the phone. He was a small, wiry man with black eyes as cold and brutal as a mortgage officer, and a bent nose and cauliflower ears from boxing in his younger days. I don't know if he was a good boxer, but he was a mean enough son of a bitch to make up for any lack of talent.

"This is Wade." His voice sounded like a cell door slamming shut. "Who's calling?"

My first thought was to hang up and try again later but I had gotten used to living on the ragged edge. "Hiya, Wade," I chirped. "This is Hollis Carpenter. Is Frank in?"

"No he ain't. And I doubt it if he'd want to talk to your goddamn ass if he was."

"My, my, my. Did he wake up on the wrong side of the bed this morning?"

"Jesus Christ. As if I ain't got enough problems without having some goddamn snotnose reporter calling up smart-assing."

"It's so good to know that in this changing world of ours, there are some constants. Whole cultures and civilizations may crumble, life as we know it may cease to exist. But when I think about it and tremble with fear, I say, Hollis, calm down. Call old Darryl Wade. He'll still be the first-class asshole he always was. You can count on it."

"Yeah, that's right — you can count on it. I'll show you how much you can count on it if I ever get the chance."

"Just try it, asshole. I'll have the biggest, meanest, bulldog lawyer in this city on your ass before you can say Marcus Vipsanius Agrippa."

"Why don't you go . . ."

"I would, but I only have a certain amount of time and I am so enjoying the mental stimulation from your advanced conversational skills. My horoscope said I should listen to mental deficients today in order to truly appreciate intelligent people."

"What are you calling up here for?" he snarled.

"The latest developments on Joe's murder."

"Yeah, that's about right. You write nasty shit about us every chance you get but when you need information, you come whining around here expecting us to just hand it to you on a silver platter. Go to hell." He slammed the phone down before I could fire off another round.

I sat staring at the phone as though it had suddenly grown a full head of hair and begun singing "Minnie the Moocher." Everybody was so testy these days. Was there a full moon?

I left the house and drove to the police station. The day was overcast and I was glad to see it. I liked the sky to do something instead of just squat there with the sun shining. It invigorated me to have dark clouds scooting around and the wind blowing. I'd noticed that the azaleas in my yard were fixing to bloom, so spring was definitely on its way. Crazy Texas weather. We had gone from a blue norther to spring in a few days. We'd probably have a few more cold spells before it was all said and done, but for the most part, winter was gone, I thought. I was wrong. It doesn't happen very often, but occasionally I am wrong.

I hopped into the Ford and headed toward the station. Downtown, I drove in the slow lane to watch the people hurrying up and down the sidewalks. I liked the activity there. A lot of the men had taken off their coats and were strolling the streets in shirts and suspenders — of course they had on pants, too. The women all looked glamorous — rushing along clutching their purses under their arms. The dress length was mid-calf and little berets seemed to be the popular fashion this winter. Neon signs flashed for you to Drink Coca-Cola at the Lamar Drugs and to Spend An Evening in Old Mexico in the Spanish Dining Room of the Lamar Hotel. The marquee at the Loews State said that *The Ghost Goes West* was playing there starring Robert Donat — 5¢ for a matinee and 15¢ for a regular show at night. *Ceiling Zero* was playing at the Metropolitan.

The thing about driving around Houston is that it's so clean and wholesome looking. All you see are office buildings, hotels, clothing stores, cafes, movie theaters, department stores. It's a deceptive facade. You have to know where to go to find the drinking and drugging and gambling and whoring. However, if you drive fifty miles to the south, you come to Galveston where it's all right out in the open — the whores, the gambling halls, the arcades, shooting galleries, strip joints — anything you want right out there for God and everybody to see. They brag about it there. In Houston, the Baptist hypocrites run the show — it's all there, and everyone does it, but we all pretend it's not and we don't. I decided I had wasted too much time so I pulled into the fast lane and buzzed on over to the police station on the corner of Preston and Caroline.

It was a five-story dark red brick building with a cement facing around the doorway with curlicue designs in the cement. As I crossed the street from the parking lot, two motorcycle patrolmen roared past me on their Harleys, their torsoes looking like inverted pyramids in their tightly-fitted coats, their jodhpurs neatly tucked into their spit-polished black boots, their faces devoid of all expression. They looked like a couple of tire tools in uniform. I flapped my hand in a wave partly to be friendly and partly because they scared the hell out of me. They nodded in unison like a couple of puppets. If I had needed a reason not to be a criminal, they were it.

The building smelled like disinfectant, old wood, and tobacco. I went through the lobby dodging streams of tobacco juice and snuff that were loosely aimed at the brass cuspidors placed at strategic intervals throughout the building. I saw a policeman who had patrolled my neighborhood for a while. A huge wad of tobacco in his left cheek disfigured his face. He grinned widely at me and a little drool of brown saliva rolled down his chin, which he wiped off with the back of his hand.

"Hello, Miss Carpenter. How you doing today?"

"Hi, Tom. I thought they'd of fired you by now."

"They did. Last week. I'm paying them to work here now. I had to get another job at night to afford it. Har! Har!" He spit into a cuspidor then laughed some more.

"They're keeping y'all busy, I see," I said after guffawing heartily along with him. Even if a cop is one of the nice ones, it's always a good idea to laugh when he makes a joke.

"Oh, yeah," he said, nodding at the groups of people in the lobby. "Happens every year at this time. The Baptist Convention is in town. You take those dried up little old men out of those dried up little old podunk towns and they go hawg wild. You'd be surprised how many Christians lose their Christianity when they get to the sinful city."

"You'd be surprised at how many Christians never had any Christianity in the first place, Tom."

"Ain't it the durn truth," he guffawed, spitting tobacco on me. I was glad I had on dark clothes.

We both turned as a policeman the size of the Empire State Building came in turkey-walking a prune in a baggy brown suit with an Adam's apple the size of a house slipper.

"Let go of me! You're making a big mistake. I'm the deacon of the Second Baptist Church of Lufkin, Texas!" he whined.

"I don't care if you're the Pope himself. Paying a prostitute to stuff a rhinestone necklace up your butt and then yank it out may be the way you wild folks carry on up in Lufkin, but that's against the law down here," the cop snarled, and marched the prune down the hall toward the booking room. The policeman glanced back over his shoulder and grinned and winked at us. I wondered how the deacon would explain his actions to the congregation.

I hoped he at least got to keep the necklace as a souvenir. Poor old bastard, it was probably hard to find somebody to shove jewelry up your ass in Lufkin.

The whole incident had cheered me up immensely. Hell, I'd already been in a good mood but I was bordering on euphoria at this point. I practically skipped up the creaky stairs to the institution-green room that was the homicide division.

Frank Brumfield motioned for me to sit on the hard wooden chair across from his regulation blond oak desk with cigarette burns and dirty words carved all over it. He looked tired and the mounds of paper work looked like they had grown there like stalagmites from drips of crime instead of water. His clothes were neatly pressed and his shoes were polished to a high shine. A cigar stuck out of the corner of his mouth.

He looked at me solemnly, saying, "I heard you called earlier. Why do you want to waste your time antagonizing that fool Darryl Wade?"

I shrugged. There really wasn't an answer for that one. Why do chickens really cross the road? Do they do it to get to the other side, or do they have a subconscious need to be flattened?

"Where is the son of a bitch, anyhow?" I asked. The homicide division was housed in one room about the same size as my living room. Beat-up desks and chairs were scattered around the room. A row of filing cabinets lined one wall, brown case folders littered on top of them. A dirty blackboard covered the northern wall, diagrams all over it and lists of what I assumed were facts of cases being currently worked on. In the bottom left-hand corner, some clown had drawn two stick figures copulating.

Smoke was coming out of one of the gray garbage cans across the room. I pointed it out to Frank and waited while he went over and poured a cup of coffee into it.

"The only thing this shit's good for," he explained. "It'll probably eat a hole in the bottom of the garbage can. Glad you came in. I was going to call you today, anyhow. Wanted to ask you what you were doing at Joe's house the other day."

I furrowed my brow in confused innocence. "I was just going to see Joe. I'd been trying to call him and got worried and went over there, is all," I said blandly. That was the truth. It wasn't all of the truth, but the part I told was true.

"And why exactly were you wanting to talk to him?" he asked me politely.

"I just wanted to talk to him. You know Joe and I were old friends, Frank. Why? Am I under suspicion?" I leaned back in the chair and crossed my ankles.

"Everybody is under suspicion," he growled, and scratched his forehead. "I know you were Joe's friend — so was I. Joe was also good friends with most of the cops on the force and they're pretty stirred up about his death. That includes the big shots upstairs and they want his murderer found. They put a lot of heat on me whenever a policeman is killed and I work extra hard. So I want to know everything Joe did and everybody he did it with, everywhere he went and what he ate. If you know something, I want you to tell me about it right now."

"I really don't know a thing, Frank." I certainly

didn't think it would behoove me to tell a policeman that one of his fellow officers might have been killed because I'd mouthed around that I was writing yet another story about police crime and corruption. Call me irresponsible but I'd rather waltz with a rattlesnake. "But if I find out anything, you'll be the first to know."

"I think you're lying to me." His voice could have been used for the skating rink at the Winter Olympics.

"Well, then," I said peevishly, "just work me over with a rubber hose, why don't you. I'm sure you have one in your desk drawer."

"I probably should, just on general principle." He sighed and ran his fingers through his salt-and-pepper hair. "Look. I'm very tired and I want to find Joe's killer and get this thing over and done with so I can go home and catch some sleep."

I nodded an understanding. I wished I could help the man. "What was he killed with?"

"I ought not to tell you anything. A .45. That's really all we know. It's probably in the bottom of the ship channel by now." He jerked a pen out of the top drawer of his desk and grabbed a piece of paper off the stack nearest him and began writing. I watched him until he looked up. "Well, are you still here? That's all. Go. If you hear anything, call me."

I stood up and gave him the thumbs up and turned to leave the room. I was a minute too late.

Darryl Wade came through the door and stood there glaring at me and blocking the exit. His white shirt and black pants were wrinkled and too big for him in the seat. His hat looked like it had lost a fight with a short-changed pimp. He planted his feet wide and crossed his arms over his chest. "Well, look who's here," he sneered. "What brings you down here?"

"The Easter Bunny. I need to put in an order for some blue eggs."

"Why don't you just —" he started to say.

"Why don't you just shut up and sit down, Wade," Frank yelled at him. "I don't want to hear it."

Wade turned white with anger and glared at me for a second longer before stepping aside to let me pass.

"What's the matter, Wade? Your undershorts too tight?" I sassed as I left the room.

I don't know what's the matter with me that I think I always have to have the last word. Cops sure aren't much help during a murder investigation, I thought grouchily as I left the building and got into my car.

I pulled the car out of the parking lot and headed for the downtown area to watch the people some more. After a while, I noticed a green Chevrolet a few cars behind me that seemed to be interested in the same sights as I was because it stayed behind me no matter which way I went. I took the next right and went two blocks and turned left and it kept coming. I finally whipped into a parking place in front of Foley Brothers Department Store and slid my hand into my pocket, and not to scratch myself, either. I had my pocket gun with me and I was going to teach the bum a whole new meaning for blowing his nose if he came near my car. The green car slowed, then kept going. A clump of other cars clustered around him so I couldn't get a look at the driver or his license plate. I pulled out of the parking place and took the next turn and wound my way out of downtown and headed back to Montrose.

Being followed was the final blow. It was time to enlist some aid. I drove directly to Gael and Katherine's house. So much had already happened that morning that I felt like I had been awake since the day after the cotton gin was invented. It was only 10:00 a.m. I pulled into the driveway behind Katherine's white Cadillac convertible.

Gael's office for the construction business was in the house, and Katherine was a freelance artist, so there was a good chance that one or both would be at home. As I walked up the steps of the gray brick bungalow I saw that Katherine had gotten her way and the trim was freshly painted green and burgundy. New awnings over the windows matched the woodwork. It looked neat and tailored. I leaned on the bell and waited.

I heard a muffled cursing of "I'm gonna kill that sonofabitch" and "I'm coming, I'm coming." Gael jerked the door open, a cup of coffee in her hand that she was quite prepared to throw in the face of the perpetrator. When she saw me her eyebrows crawled down and met over her nose.

"Oh, it's just you," she muttered quietly, scowled, and motioned for me to come in.

"Got any more coffee?"

"You know where it is. Go get some," she growled and shuffled sleepily to the couch.

I went into the kitchen for the coffee, then joined her in the living room.

"That a new couch?"

"Re-upholstered."

"Oh. Where's Katherine?"

"In the bedroom exercising. Jinx is in there with her," Gael said, sipping and smoking. Jinx was their dog.

"Maybe I'll go in there and watch," I said innocently.

"I wouldn't do that if I were you; she doesn't have any clothes on."

"Why do you think I wanted to go in there?"

She finally began to wake up and grin. "What are you doing out and about so early? I thought you'd be sleeping until noon since you don't have to go in to work. Hell, take advantage of it while it lasts."

"Places to go, things to do, people to see," I said airily, waving my hand like a symphony conductor.

"Such as?"

We heard Katherine's footsteps heading toward the living room.

"Hollis is here. You'd better put a robe on," Gael said, raising her voice but not fast enough to prevent Katherine from opening the door, seeing me, squealing, and slamming the door.

I didn't have enough class to look in the other direction, so I caught a brief glimpse of long Texas legs. I wiggled my eyebrows up and down and smirked lasciviously for Gael's benefit. She grinned and flicked ashes into the crystal ashtray on the coffee table and said, "She's probably too horrified to come back out."

Katherine, wearing a turquoise satin bathrobe, sailed into the living room and stuck her tongue out. "I can't believe y'all let me walk out here naked like that," she said. Only when she said it, it sounded like, "Ah caint buhlieve y'all let me walk out here nekked like thayut."

"I'm certainly not going to do anything as foolish as stop a good-looking woman from parading in front of me naked if she wants to," I said, and kissed her cheek as she leaned down to hug me. She giggled and dealt a loving blow to my head that made my ears ring for thirty minutes.

"What are you up to today?" she asked as she settled onto the couch beside Gael and adjusted her bathrobe so I couldn't peek. Before I could answer, she turned to Gael with a look that only the royal family and very good-looking women use. "Babe, would you please get me some coffee?"

Gael rolled her eyes at me and I laughed as she went to the kitchen. There was no doubt in anyone's mind that she would go and get the coffee. There was no room in that regal look for refusal.

When she returned, I told them everything that had happened with Cotton and Tully.

"I can't believe you went up to his hotel room by yourself. What if he'd had a gun. He might have killed you," Katherine scolded.

"He wasn't in any shape to kill anybody," I pointed out.

"You know what I mean," Katherine said dangerously, and began looking for objects to hurl. She picked up a small bronze dancing lady on a marble base and eyed it, calculating whether the cost was worth the satisfaction of braining me. She finally put it back down, picked up a throw pillow, and waited for the next opportunity. “I just don’t see how you can stand this kind of thing. Your job has always had you chasing down criminals and always seeing so much blood and gore and now you’re doing it and not even getting paid for it!”

“Oh, I’m okay with it unless they start picking their noses. I can pretty much handle anything but that,” I said indelicately. The pillow whizzed through the air but I ducked it easily.

“You shouldn’t be running around out there by yourself,” she said emphatically.

“Oh, Hollis can take care of herself. It’s the criminals who need to be worried,” Gael said from the cloud of cigarette smoke surrounding her head.

“Sure I can,” I chirped confidently.

“No, you can’t. It’s too dangerous — all those lunatics out there breaking in your house and killing everybody, and God knows what else. Gael will go with you.” Which was exactly what I had hoped she would say.

Gael looked at her then looked at me and sighed and said that Katherine was right. “You don’t have enough sense to stay out of trouble.”

“Well, I hate to impose, but if you insist.” I smiled ingratiatingly.

“You are up to something,” Katherine said, looking at me suspiciously. “I can tell by that innocent look on your face. Let’s have it.”

“Unh unh,” I said and stared at the ceiling.

“Yes, you are,” she accused, looking at me with gimlet eyes and waving another pillow.

I kept looking at the ceiling. Gael was still only

half awake, although she prided herself on being able to operate on three or four hours of sleep a night. She sipped her coffee and blinked occasionally.

Katherine began the tortuous third degree. "Did you make some fudge and not save any for me?"

"No."

"You've got a girlfriend!" she shrieked, and banged her hand on the sofa.

Gael snorted like a dumptruck backfiring and mashed out her cigarette, her eyes beginning to show signs of something that could conceivably be called life. She shuffled into the kitchen for more coffee. She came back running her fingers through her hair and scratching her head to jumpstart her brain.

"Give me a hint. Is it about a person, place, or thing?" Katherine kept on. It was driving her crazy and I loved it.

"It has something to do with Lily Delacroix. She either has seen her or is going to," Gael said matter-of-factly.

Katherine's mouth dropped open and she looked at Gael as though she were Harry Houdini back from the grave. "Is that right?" she yelped.

I just grinned.

"Now, how did you know that?" she asked and whopped Gael for a change. At least half a cup of scalding coffee went into Gael's lap. She jumped off the couch and brushed her legs, wincing with pain.

"I could tell by the way she talked about her the other night when we were at her house. I knew something was bound to happen." Gael shrugged, mopping her lap with a napkin.

"I just hate it when you're right," Katherine complained. "It makes you so hard to live with."

"All right, tell me all about it," Katherine said, turning to me and unconsciously clutching the lapels of her robe.

So I told her all about it. She rolled her eyes to indicate that I had offended her moral sensibilities when I got to the part about kissing Lily.

"That poor woman. Here she had poured her heart out to you — the one person in this whole city she felt she could talk to, and what do you do? You maul her. I don't know what's the matter with you." Katherine sniffed, affronted.

"Don't pay any attention to Katherine," Gael said. "The last time I tried to tell Katherine about something that was bothering me, she told me to take my feelings and shove them up my ass."

"Baby!" Katherine shrieked indignantly. "My mind got sidetracked while you were talking. I didn't know what I was saying!"

That was a problem in their relationship — Katherine had a short attention span and Gael was long-winded — it made for some mighty interesting conversations. I could tell Katherine was immensely pleased with herself, nonetheless. She decided to get the focus off herself. "So when are you going to see this person again?"

"Tonight. I'm supposed to meet her in front of the Rice Hotel. Benny Goodman's playing on the Roof."

"Well, I hope you know what you're doing. Her being a married woman and all."

"I know, I know, I know. I've thought about all

of that. I've just decided to take it as it comes and not worry about it. Hell, I could be run over by a bus tomorrow. You never know."

"I don't mind if you get run down by a bus, but I hate to think of you getting gunned down by the mob. Gael will be your bodyguard."

To Katherine, Gael somehow seemed omnipotent, omniscient and bulletproof. It didn't seem to occur to Katherine that if Gael was with me, she could be in danger. I didn't bother to point this out to her because I needed all the help I could get. At five-feet-five and 125 pounds, Gael wasn't exactly what most people would call an intimidating henchman, but she could look mean when she had to. She was better than nothing. I wasn't sure how the two of us would hold up in a gun or knife fight, but if anybody wanted to debate an issue, we'd roll all over 'em.

"So, where are y'all going today?" Katherine asked.

"First to Susie Noble's, then I'm not sure. I've got to find out as much as I can, as fast as I can."

"Well that figures. I let you two go off by yourselves and you head straight for a whorehouse."

"I just need to find out if Joe was there the night he got killed," I explained. "Maybe he said something to Susie or one of the girls that might help find out who killed him."

"Oh, sure." Katherine's voice reeked with sarcasm. "Gael has done several construction jobs for that chippy. The way she calls over here all the time, I think she's attracted to Gael."

I could tell Katherine really didn't believe that at all. She was just saying it to put Gael on the defensive. Women are like that. They like to stockpile ammunition in case of war. That way, if Katherine went out and spent too much money on a dress, for instance, she could use Susie as a red herring to cloud the issue. It's a way to take the heat off themselves.

"You want to go with us?" I asked her.

"No, I can't. Sakowitz Brothers is having a one-day sale," she said as though she had no choice in the matter. Katherine's philosophy was that a person had absolute free will until there was a big sale at a fashionable department store, then predestination prevailed.

"Oh, shit," Gael muttered under her breath, as she walked toward the bedroom to get dressed.

"What did you say, sweetie?" Katherine called in an angelic voice while winking wickedly at me. "I just need a few little things."

She had that same look on her face that Napoleon probably got whenever Russia was mentioned. That look usually meant at least two new outfits.

Finally Gael came out ready to leave. She wouldn't go out of the house unless she felt perfectly dressed. Her clothes had to be starched and ironed and her shoes had to shine.

Katherine put her arms around her and told her how good she looked. It didn't take much to play Gael like a baby grand piano. And Katherine was a concert pianist when it came to Gael's ego.

Gael beamed brightly. "I'm ready," she said, as she turned her collar up around her neck to look flashy.

"Try not to buy out the store," I admonished

Katherine, just to work Gael's nerves. Katherine's laughter sounded demented as it followed us out to the car. Gael blanched and I could tell she was mentally kissing the old bank account goodbye. But she sauntered around to her side of the car, got in and immediately pushed in the cigarette lighter. I backed out of the driveway, still grinning at Katherine's nonsense.

"You really shouldn't encourage her, you know," Gael said sternly.

"Does Susie have a thing for you?" I asked.

"Nah, she just likes to have somebody she can talk to sometimes. She likes politics. She combs the newspaper every day soaking up world news. She likes to talk about how small the world has become with the advent of the telephone and telegraph. We talk about how the whole world will be like one big country one day. Everybody will be just alike. It's inevitable." Gael was on a roll, her hands gesturing in small tight circles, the gestures broken only by the motion of taking a drag off her Camel cigarette. She held forth on the subject as I drove down Richmond Road and headed toward Caroline Street.

When Gael got on a roll, it was hard to interrupt. About thirty-five percent was bullshit and twelve to fifteen percent was opinion, but the rest was fact. And it wasn't worth the effort to go study the subject to see which was which.

"It all started with the China Clipper," she lectured between puffs on the Camel. "On November 22, when the first Clipper left San Francisco for Manila, the ocean barriers shrank to a minor inconvenience. Now, all of the capitals of the world are within commuting distance instead of just those of the Caribbean and South America." She had worked her way through the shrinking of the world, Huey Long's assassination, Mussolini's invasion of Ethiopia, and was warming up on the subject of the luxury of travel by rail when we turned onto Caroline and drove up to Susie's brothel. I was sorry the trip was over since I was picking up some great shit that I wouldn't have to read about.

I said, "So, Susie likes to discuss all this stuff? You know somebody for fifteen years and you learn something about them you'd never suspect. Fascinating. I've known killers who collect butterflies and do needlepoint, boxers who secretly want to join the ballet, mobsters who cry at the opera. I'm telling you, it's a strange world."

Susie's house was a dark red brick Gothic horror with gables and leaded glass windows. The yard was completely covered with bushes and shrubs and trees. Susie said it cut down on yard work and kept people from sneaking outside to make whoopee in the yard and upsetting the neighbors.

We went up to the heavy wooden door and rang the bell. A small peephole door at eye level opened. I told the eyeball who I was and the little door slammed shut. A young woman of about nineteen threw open the front door. All she wore was a pink see-through negligee and a pout. There was nothing but a satisfied groan left to the imagination. Her brown hair was pinned loosely to the top of her head.

"Hi ya, Gael," she said breathily and flared her nostrils. She reached out and touched Gael's crotch. "Gee, I like those pants."

I grinned tightly and raised my eyebrows at Gael. "What gives?"

She grinned sheepishly. "They just like to do shit like that around here. Habit."

"Funny, nobody ever did it to me."

We walked out of the foyer into a room where the customers could sit and drink with the girls while waiting to go upstairs. Some people did just drop by for a drink and to visit with the other patrons. Most men figured they were safe from prying eyes and Susie protected them from gossip. If she ever found out that anybody in her employ had been out flapping their gums and being indiscreet, they were fired immediately and a big bouncer named Bitsy hauled them down to the Greyhound station and stuck them on the first bus out of town to anywhere.

The room was off-white and so was everything in it, down to the padded leather stools and the padded leather bar. A crystal chandelier hung in the middle of the room, and all of the other light fixtures had pink bulbs in them, an idea Susie had gotten from Earthman's Funeral Home when she went to pay her last respects to Legs Greer — one of the greatest second story men in Texas. She figured if pink lights could make corpses look alive, think what they could do for whores. And they did seem to work, I noticed as I glanced at myself in a mirror. I made a mental note to pick some up for my bedroom. The customers' room was cozy and intimate but empty at that time of day. A bartender was polishing the glasses and bottles behind the bar.

We went down the hall, which was also off-white and lit with pink bulbs, and banged on the third door. A lilting Irish voice told us to come in.

Susie sat at a roll-top desk doing her book work. We waited until she reached a stopping point. She had on a pair of bifocals which she quickly jerked off and stuffed into a drawer when she saw us standing there.

"Well, Hollis, Gael. What in the world brings you two over here this morning?" She walked over and sat on the gray divan with large pink roses all over it, and gestured us to the small gray wingbacks that faced it.

The room was painted a pale green and was strictly business-like, nothing personal in it except for a small tea set on the coffee table that had been given to her as a child. I think she kept it as a reminder of her lost innocence. She had told me once that whenever she felt cold and hard and callous, she would lock the door and have a tea party. She would serve herself tea and crackers just as she had as a child until she broke down and cried, then she could go on with her business for a while.

Susie was slender and petite, with curly red hair and green eyes. Her smile was impish and seductive at the same time. Her face reminded me of a Renaissance painting. Her personality was subtly sensual, and I was never quite sure if she was flirting with me. When you talked to her, she looked you dead in the eyes and listened carefully to everything you said as though you were the most important person in the world. I could understand why some men would pay for that. She had been involved since the age of sixteen with a handsome con artist named Leslie Bosarge who had taught her a few cons and the art of picking pockets. Bo was a drifter and he came and went whenever the urge struck. That was okay with Susie, she liked her freedom, too.

Her green dress matched her eyes. She sat on the couch with her feet tucked under her and her left arm resting casually on the back of the couch. I don't care who you were, or who you were involved with, when you were around Susie, it was hard not to fall under her spell. I glanced at Gael and hoped I didn't have the same sappy look on my face, although I was pretty sure I did.

"Did Gene ever get by here yesterday to install that light in the bathroom for you? I told him to do it first thing," Gael said.

"Yes, he did. It looks wonderful," Susie said, smiling and twinkling her eyes at Gael.

Gael stuck a cigarette in her mouth and picked up a box of wooden matches from a bowl on the Duncan Phyfe coffee table. She lit the cigarette, drew on it until the tip glowed like a virgin drinking cheap champagne, and slowly shook the match out. Every move she made was slower and more sensual than usual.

A snort slipped out of me before I could stifle it. Her eyes cut through me like a switchblade through a watermelon and then went back to Susie.

"I've been thinking about redoing the poker room upstairs, maybe knocking out a wall to that adjoining room and enlarging it. What do you think?" Susie asked Gael.

"I don't think you ought to make it any bigger. Psychologically it's about the right size. We might paint it and a few things like that, though. I can go look around while I'm here and see what we can do."

Susie nodded and Gael stalked like a panther from the room.

I skipped the niceties and went straight to the heart of the matter.

"I guess you heard about Joe Mahan?"

"Yes. A terrible thing! Who in the world would want to hurt Joe? Do they know who did it yet?"

I shook my head. "I was wondering if he was over here that night."

She leaned back and stared off into the distance, biting the inside corner of her mouth as she thought. "Let me see. Joe hasn't been here in at least two weeks."

I was shocked. As far as I knew, he had never gone more than two days without dropping by Susie's. "You've got to be kidding! What did he do — buy himself a vacuum cleaner and paint lips on the hose and name it Joan?"

"He would have been better off if he had," Susie laughed. "He got himself a girlfriend. As a matter of fact, he took her from here. She'd been working for me about five months. Joe saw her regularly and decided he was in love with her. The boob even asked her to marry him. God knows why — if I hadn't needed somebody desperately after Sandra left here last summer, I wouldn't have hired the girl in the first place. I wish I never had. She just laughed at him and said she didn't want to go live in some shack on the East Side and wash his dirty underwear. He'd get drunk and beg her. The big slob had it bad."

"Joe's brain always was in his dick. Where is this vision of loveliness and purity?"

"Her name is Colette. Joe took her out of here and put her up in an apartment of her own. She wouldn't even let the old fool move in with her."

I was dumbfounded. "Joe couldn't afford to keep a mouse in a cage, much less a woman in an apartment. What the hell was he thinking?"

"Oh, he came into some money a couple of weeks ago. His rich aunt finally kicked off and left it all to him. He came in here spending like a drunken sailor on shore leave and that's when she agreed to go with him. I tried like hell to talk him out of it, but he wouldn't listen," Susie said quietly. "Would you like a bottle of Co' Cola?"

I said I'd love a bottle and Susie went to the kitchen where she kept a huge wooden tub of Coca-Colas and beer iced down for her customers. My mouth was dry and my face felt like a pin cushion. I felt sick. Joe didn't have any rich relatives, dead or alive. There was more likelihood of my getting an urgent call from Franklin Roosevelt to sing the National Anthem at a state dinner than there was of Joe inheriting money.

Susie came back with two bottles of Coca-Cola. I took a sip to fuel my brain, then asked, "Where is the girl living?"

"I can't remember. She dropped by here about a week ago in new clothes and said Joe was going to buy her a new car pretty soon. I was too disgusted to talk to her, but some of the girls did. Let me get one of them." She went to the door and yelled down the hall for someone named Brandy.

The pouty girl in the negligee flounced into the room. "Whatcha want, Susie?"

"First of all, I want you to quit running around here naked. How many times do I have to tell you I don't want you girls to come out of your rooms undressed. This is a class joint, get it? Now, do you remember where Colette moved to?"

Brandy bit her lip and wrinkled her forehead. I hoped she didn't bust a blood vessel with the tremendous mental strain.

"Wasn't it the Plaza? Yeah, I'm pretty sure that was it — over on Montrose Boulevard."

"All right. That's all. Now scoot, and get dressed and remember what I said."

Brandy smiled blankly and I knew she had already forgotten what Susie had told her. She wiggled her fingers in what she probably interpreted as a sexy wave and left the room, wagging her tail behind her.

Susie sighed deeply and looked tired. "I hate yelling at them, but sometimes they just don't seem to understand anything else. I think I need to take a vacation. Get away from this dump for a month or so. Maybe Florida. This town gives me the blues this time of the year."

"Yeah. I know exactly what you mean. I guess I'd better run, Susie. Let you get back to work. Oh, by the way, do you know a little albino-looking weasel named Cotton Peeples?"

"Sure. Who doesn't know the little loser. Why?"

"I've got to find him. You don't happen to know where he might be, do you?"

"No, but if I hear anything, I'll let you know. What's all this about, Hollis?"

"I don't know. But I sure aim to find out."

She looked puzzled, told me to be careful, and hugged me goodbye.

We walked down the hall together and found Gael sitting at the bar telling the bartender the proper recipe for a Planter's Punch. She and Susie discussed the changes for the poker room, haggled over the color and price, then we left.

Cranking the car, I told Gael everything I had found out. I headed back toward Montrose Boulevard. When we got to the Main Street intersection, I asked Gael if she wanted to stop for something to eat.

"Sure," she cut her eyes at me. "As long as it isn't a hot dog."

I took a left on Main heading south. We passed the Warwick Hotel and my heart fluttered, thinking about being there with Lily the night before. I got so distracted, I almost wiped out a family crossing the street on their way to the zoo and Gael yelled at me to keep my mind on my driving.

Ye Olde College Inn was a one-story white stucco building with dark green shutters closed over the windows. A sign to the right of the front door said that Duncan Hines recommended this restaurant for travelers. Duncan Hines didn't have to recommend it to me, I knew the food was good. The cafe sat on the edge of the campus of Rice Institute, and families visiting their sons and daughters often brought them here to eat. It was also a popular place for the doctors and lawyers who lived in Southhampton and West University Place. I had a sneaky feeling that more criminals were tried over the chicken fried steak here than at the courthouse.

After lunch Gael insisted on driving. She said she didn't want to be unreasonable, but she'd like to make it home with all of her limbs. I was too stuffed to duel verbally, so I filed the insult away for later. I leaned back in the seat to enjoy the ride. Gael whipped the car around like a tango dancer. All she needed was a rose clamped between her teeth. As we whizzed past Hermann Park, I noticed green buds on the pecan trees. We were going so fast we probably caused the water in Hermann Pond to run backwards for three days afterwards. We soared up Montrose Boulevard, passing everyone else like they were rooted to the spot, and screeched to a halt on a side street by the Plaza Hotel. I felt enlightened now that I knew Gael's definition of safe driving. The next time I got behind the wheel, I was going to do everything I could to make her feel twice as safe as she just had me.

We walked into the cool, dark lobby of the hotel and I told Gael that I probably should talk to Colette alone so she wouldn't feel ganged-up on. She agreed and moseyed happily toward the bar.

I went to the front desk to talk to the clerk — a greasy creep with a shiny pencil mustache. He played dumb about the girl until I slipped him a bill and he opened his beak and sang like a canary. She was registered under the name of Colette Chateau in apartment 403. He would have told me her favorite color, favorite song, and her bra size if I'd had the time to listen and the money to spend.

"Colette Chateau. Jesus Christ," I grumbled to myself as I rode the elevator to four and knocked on her door. A radio was playing Benny Goodman loudly from within. A cheap, tinny voice screeched, "Come on in, Sugar, it's open." So Sugar went on in since it was open. The way I looked at it was that I could be "Sugar" just as well as anyone else.

Colette obviously didn't look at it the same way I did. She was posing in the middle of the room in a corset, black fishnets, and high heels. She was about twenty-five and her face was as fresh as the lettuce in my icebox left over from the diet I had started on New Year's Day and quit New Year's night. When she had poured the bleach on her hair, she'd been reaching for the color of the moon, but her grasp had only gotten as far as a hay stack on the King Ranch. Actually, she would have done better just sticking straw on her head and skipping the bleach. Her eyebrows were drawn on like Jean Harlow's but all resemblance ended there. "Who're you?" she shrieked in a voice that made a fishwife sound like Dorothy Lamour singing the baby to sleep. She grabbed up the shiny red kimono lying on the chair beside her and put it on.

"My name's Hollis Carpenter, Miss Chateau." I tried not to flinch as I uttered the name — hers, not mine. "I was a friend of Joe Mahan's."

"Yeah, Joe mentioned you before. Pleasedtameetcha." She looked at me like I was a grease spot on a new suit. Which was okay with me. I would have felt bad if she had liked me.

"I thought I'd come by and offer my condolences. Let you know that if I can be of any help, please feel free to call me. I'm sure you miss him a lot."

Sure. Like a wino misses purple snakes and pink elephants. She had wasted as much time grieving about Joe as Al Capone had spent in Sunday School.

"Yeah, sure. I miss him a lot. He was a swell guy. Listen, I got somewhere I need to be in a few minutes and I ain't even dressed yet, so if you don't mind . . . Maybe we can get together some other time and talk about Joe."

I sat on the new, cheap Early American orange chair that matched the new, cheap Early American sofa and noticed a cigar stub in the souvenir ashtray of the Grand Canyon on the cheap maple veneer Early American cocktail table.

"It must have been awful for you finding out about Joe like that," I said, ignoring her invitation to leave. "How did you find out about it, by the way?"

"What?"

"I said how did you find out about Joe getting killed? Who told you about it?" I was poking in the dark, grabbing at straws, trying to get her to talk.

"I don't see what business it is of yours who told me about Joe," she sassed.

"Look, Miss Chateau," I began, gritting my teeth at having to lower myself to say the ridiculous name. Colette Chateau. I guessed they were the only French words she'd ever heard. "It probably isn't any of my business who told you about Joe, but did you ever stop and think that the person who told you might have killed him? And if that's true, your not telling me is covering for a murderer. That makes you an accessory after the fact. That's about ten to fifteen ironing striped uniforms in the women's unit up in Huntsville."

I was going at her in an authoritative, rapid-fire, no-room-for-argument kind of voice. Hoping she couldn't think fast enough to recognize a giant pile of bullshit when somebody dumped it in her living room. My face was as serious as a lawyer's fee.

"Ha, ha, ha," she sneered. "Who do you think you're dealing with? I ain't some dumb hick you can come in here and browbeat. A cop told me about Joe."

"Oh, yeah? Which one?" I asked suspiciously.

"Darryl Wade. That's who, Miss Smarty Pants."

Swell. It would have saved me some time if Frank Brumfield had told me about this woman that morning while I was digging information out of him. I wondered what else he knew that he'd held out. Some reporter I was.

"Was Joe up here the night he was killed?"

"Yeah, he left about midnight."

"Why didn't he spend the night?"

"That's none of your business. I don't have to talk to you."

"I'm just trying to find out if he might have told you that he had some place to go or somebody to meet. Believe me, I'm not trying to pry into your love life with Joe. As a matter of fact, I can't think of anything I would care less about hearing."

"No. He didn't say he was going to meet somebody. And I don't know who killed Joe. You don't think I'd a told the cops that morning if I had?" She glanced nervously at the cheap Early American clock on the wall.

"I heard Joe inherited some money. Do you know how much it was or who it was from?"

She walked over to an ornately carved shelf and

began fiddling with a souvenir outhouse with the door open and a small surprised boy sitting in it. She picked it up and moved it over an inch closer to the chalk Horn of Plenty. I really appreciated her taste in decorating.

"If Joe had wanted you to know any of that, he'd a told you. Now, I really have to get dressed to go somewhere and I'd appreciate it if you'd kindly get the hell out of my house."

"All right, Miss Chateau." I was sure that given an hour or two of practice in front of a mirror, I could make the name roll off my tongue quite naturally. "I'm going to leave my card here on your table. If you remember anything that might be of help, or decide you just need a friend to talk to, give me a call."

"I don't think that'll happen, so you can just take your card with you."

I left the card where it lay on the table. I stood up and looked slowly around the room. "You like your place?"

"Yeah, it's all right."

"You know, for the last thirty years of his life, every time Joe made love to a woman, he had to worry about somebody banging on the door and yelling 'time's up.' I guess he finally got tired of it — enough to set you up in this place. I don't know yet what he had to do to afford it, but I'm sure as hell going to find out. I just hope it was worth it for him."

"Get out!" she screamed and hurled the little outhouse at me. I was running into the hurling girls today. Thank God for all the practice I'd had with Katherine. I ducked it with the ease of a heavyweight champ and it shattered harmlessly inches from my head.

I left since there didn't seem to be anything else to say. I closed the door and made a lot of noise walking down the hall. Halfway to the elevator, I turned and tiptoed back to the door. I could hear her on the telephone, but I couldn't understand what she was saying until she screamed "Goddamn" and slammed it down.

I rushed back to the elevator, pushed the button, and stared at the ceiling, whistling innocently. I don't know why I did it, there's nothing more guilty-looking than somebody staring at the ceiling whistling innocently. The elevator swished up like a queen flirting with a sailor and I rode it back down to the lobby. There was a phone booth tucked discreetly in the back of the lobby and I decided to do something smart for a change and use it to save myself some driving. I dug into my pants pocket. No nickels. I ankled on over to the front desk and handed the creep a dollar. He was fast. He had it in his pocket before I could even open my mouth to ask for change. I smiled a mean smile and shook my head motioning for him to give me back my money.

"Not this time, handsome. I just need some nickels for the phone." I stuck my hand out, palm up, and wiggled my fingers for him to hurry with the change. His face fell like a boxer taking a dive in the third round. He dragged the bill reluctantly back out of his pocket. It took a long time, as though the dollar had attached itself like a barnacle to the hull of a ship.

I went to the phone booth and shut the door.

The booth smelled like old cigars and old sweat and old disappointments from dialing lovers who should have been at home at three o'clock in the morning, but weren't. I called Pete at the American Brotherhood Club to see if Cotton was there, but Pete said he hadn't been there since the day before. And no, he had no idea where Cotton was flopping or where else he hung out. I thanked him and dragged out the Yellow Pages and started calling downtown hotels that were the sort Cotton might stay at, the kind of hotels where you had to pay extra for the bedbugs. The rooms without the bedbugs came with lice and fleas. I called them all but no luck.

There were twenty-three listings for beer gardens and twenty-two taverns in the book and my nickels were running low, so I just called the ones in the immediate downtown area, also without luck. I was flipping the pages and putting another nickel in the slot when I glanced across the lobby to see if Gael had come out of the bar. My mind was in a million different places at once and I almost didn't take it in that the man crossing the lobby toward the elevator was Darryl Wade. I slammed the phone down and ducked in the booth as he looked around the lobby, waiting for the elevator. I don't know why I ducked, I just did. Maybe just because I hated the bastard so much, maybe because I didn't want him to get back at me for smart-mouthing him.

He got on the elevator and as soon as the door closed, I retrieved my nickel from the coin slot and galloped across the lobby to the elevator. The needle over the door floated slowly from one to four and stopped. I wondered if he was there on official police business. Sure he was — and Clark Gable wore pink pinafores around his house to relax.

I hadn't done my knee any favors running across the lobby, so I was limping slightly when I went back to the front desk. The clerk's lips were pinched tightly together as he watched me coming toward him.

"Does that man come in here very often?"

"What man? I didn't see a man."

"The one in the ill-fitting, wrinkled black suit with the hat that looked too big, and the face that looked like a chicken wing after the preacher got through gnawing on it. That man."

The clerk smiled despicably, stuck his hand out, palm up, and wiggled his fingers at me. The pupils in his eyes were little black dollar signs.

I breathed deeply, and silently asked God for the strength to refrain from ramming my foot so far up this guy's ass that a surgeon would have to separate us. I dug into my pocket, got out a dollar bill and slid it across the desk at him. He snatched it up and opened his trap. "He comes up to see Miss Chateau a lot. He usually spends the night after the other john leaves."

I guessed the other "john" in question was Joe. It made me sick. I wanted to go home and take a bath, but there probably wasn't enough soap in the world to make me feel clean.

I crossed the lobby and stepped down into the bar. The room was white with dark woodwork and no windows. Gael was behind the bar shaking a chrome and red glass cocktail shaker. The bartender stood beside her nodding and taking notes as she talked.

"You want a champagne cocktail? It's the latest from the Savoy," she told me through lips that clamped a cigarette. She squinted knowledgeably through the plume of smoke from her Camel.

"How do you know all that shit?" I propped a foot on the brass railing along the bottom of the bar and leaned on an elbow to watch her shake. The wooden ceiling fans turned slowly and blew the fronds gently on the palms scattered throughout the bar.

A handful of dedicated drinkers had gathered around to watch her lecture. She poured several cocktails into champagne glasses, passed them out to all of the observers, and handed me the one with the most in it. I grinned gratefully until she pointed at me and magnanimously announced, "The drinks are on her." The moochers raised their glasses in a toast.

I sipped my drink and mulled over the recent events, and, although I still couldn't make sense of it all, it was sure getting interesting. I still didn't have enough information and didn't know where to go to get it so I figured all I could do was run around town sticking my spoon in and stirring as fast and as much as I could. It was going to have to be a mighty big spoon.

Gael had worked her way through the latest in drink crazes in all of the major hotels in London and was starting on the ones from the most popular night clubs in Hollywood before I yanked her out of the bar. She had totted up quite a tab for me by that time but as she pointed out, everybody in there would be my friend for life.

Huge, chunky, pewter clouds were moving across the sky from the north as we walked to the car. It would be raining by nightfall.

Gael drove while I told her about Colette. The good thing about Gael was that, as much as she liked to talk, she also liked to listen, and you only had to tell her something once. I finished and gave her time to digest it.

"What now?" she asked, finally.

"You tell me. I'm at a dead end. The only thing I can think to do is to keep looking for Cotton Peeples."

"Where do we go for that?"

"Let's just ride around downtown for a while. See if we see him on the streets anywhere. If we see someplace promising, we can stop."

We cruised up Montrose and cut across at Alabama and went over to Main Street, then turned north and drifted up and down the streets. Occasionally I would see a newsboy or shoeshine man I knew and Gael would park the car and wait while I talked to them and put the word out that I needed information on Joe and Cotton. I saw a couple of coke heads and numbers runners and small-time hoods that I had gotten information from before and let them know there was money in it for them if they got anything, but it needed to be soon.

"Where the hell do you meet these people?" Gael growled as she pulled out into the traffic after I had talked to a particularly disgusting hood who had leaned over right in the middle of a sentence and blown his nose with his fingers.

"Well, what the hell kind of people do you think I'd know in my line of work? Crimes aren't usually committed by debutantes. If I want to find a pitiful little drunken crook, I'm not likely to get information on him at the River Oaks Country Club, now am I?"

"Probably depends on who you talk to. I'll bet at least half the fortunes in River Oaks were built on illegal activities."

Every now and then we stopped at a pool hall or gin joint and went in looking for Cotton. A few people knew him or knew of him, but nobody knew where to find him. Nobody seemed to know where he was working or if he was working.

A couple of times, I thought I noticed a green sedan following us, but I pointed it out to Gael and she lost it in the traffic. We finally decided to give up on Cotton and went over to St. Joseph's Infirmary to put the squeeze on Tully Kirk. I didn't think he knew anything, but it was worth a shot. When we got to the information desk at the hospital, a nun with a face that could have been used to dig the Panama Canal told us that Tully had skipped out that afternoon.

"I want to know where all those sweet, angelic nuns are that you read about," I complained as we got back in the car. "All of the ones I've ever seen look like they could go bear hunting with a switch."

"Shit," Gael snorted with the authority of one who had attended Catholic girls' school, "they don't need a switch to go bear hunting. The switch is just for fun. They could rip a bear's lips off with their bare hands."

"Was that a deliberate play on words?"

She shook her head and whipped the car around

an old Ford truck with about sixteen construction workers sitting in the back grinning at us. It looked like each one of them was missing at least two thirds of his teeth. We came to a four-way stop and the truck pulled up beside us.

The men waved and shouted obscene suggestions.

We gave them the bird and drove off. They laughed loudly and whistled.

"I never have my sawed-off shotgun when I need it," Gael growled.

Since we were both tired of driving around but getting nowhere, we headed back toward Montrose. I asked, "Think Katherine's home yet?"

"God knows. You know how she loves to shop. Especially when she gets a snooty sales clerk." Gael's face tightened like a dried sponge and her eyes looked off into the distance. She always got that look remembering the only time she had gone shopping with Katherine. They had been shopping all day and Gael nearly had her out of the store when Katherine spotted a purse in a case and stopped to look at it. The clerk was a bitch, so Katherine started talking in a hick voice when she looked at the price tag. "Thur's a mistake hyur. This says a hunnerd and twenty bucks. You must mean twelve." And the clerk said, "There is no mistake. The bag is alligator." And Katherine said, "I don't care if it dances like Ginger Rogers, this purse ain't worth a hunnerd and twenty bucks. Why it ain't even got any gold on it. Whur's the gold?" Then she waved at Gael and screamed, "Myrtle, git your butt over hyur and look at this purse!" Gael was trying to hide under the perfume counter by that time. The clerk took the purse back and said, "Of course, this purse is not for everyone." And Katherine haughtily replied, "Yes, and I see you don't have one either, you piss-ant!" And then she sailed out of the store, revitalized. Gael had whimpered all the way home.

Katherine's car was in the driveway by the time we got to the house. Katherine was lounging on the sofa with her shoes kicked off and her feet up on the coffee table. Boxes and bags were strewn and stacked around the room.

"A successful day?" Gael grinned and kissed her.

"A very successful day, thank you. It was exhausting, but someone had to do it. How about y'all? Anything interesting?"

"A few things," I said and told her about our day. She picked up a shaker of martinis and poured us each one as I talked.

Gael sat on the sofa beside Katherine and lit a cigarette. Katherine snuggled closely up to her and laid her head on her shoulder. "I love you, Baby." She batted her eyes until they created a breeze.

"I must have bought you something really expensive today," Gael said, and eyed her suspiciously.

"Oh, you did."

"Then I don't want to know about it. Just don't even tell me about it," Gael groaned.

"Listen, before this thing turns into a real bloodbath, I'm going to run on home," I interrupted.

"Don't run off," Katherine objected. "You just got here!"

"I've got to go walk Anice and I'm going to try to take a nap before I go out tonight."

"Oh, yes. The date! You be good and have fun tonight, and try to keep your hands to yourself, for a change," she said as they walked me to the door.

"Don't worry! If I don't have a stroke before I get there, I'll have a great time."

When I got home, I walked Anice, who barked ferociously at everyone we encountered. It always thrilled her when people acted scared of her so I had trained everyone in the neighborhood to say "OOOOOHHH" whenever they saw her coming. Several people screamed in terror as we passed, so Anice was positively skipping by the time we got back home.

We ate some gingersnaps as I tore hysterically around the house running the vacuum, changing the sheets, hiding the dirty dishes in the cabinet, running a dust rag over everything. I looked around the house with an overwhelming discontent and wanted to rip out the carpet and pitch out all of my furniture. My channel-backed couch and matching chair were covered in black to go with the black leather and chrome lounge. What in the hell could I possibly have been thinking when I had decorated the place and painted the walls red? I wasn't much better than Colette Chateau.

I turned on the chrome torchiere lamp in the corner and saw the brown stripe of dirt that went all the way around the bottom of the couch where Anice wiped her beard after she ate. She would go to the couch, hold her face against it and run all the way around it, then turn around and press the other side against the couch and do it all again in reverse. It was also how she dried herself after a bath. I turned that lamp off and turned on a small table lamp that didn't illuminate so much dirt.

After I finished cleaning, I saw that I still had two hours before I needed to be at the Rice Hotel. I rushed into the bedroom, ripped off my clothes and threw myself into the bed. I closed my eyes for three seconds before they flew back open and I stared in a blind panic wondering what the hell I thought I was doing. That woman couldn't possibly be interested in me. I took a few deep breaths and closed my eyes again. I thrashed around in the bed like a machine harvesting wheat until I couldn't stand it any more and got up and went into the bathroom.

I took a bath, then a shower, then got dressed and changed clothes three times. I rushed frantically around the house again, straightening up the bed which I had messed up trying to take a nap, and rehanging the clothes I had pitched around the room in a fit of dissatisfaction with the way I looked.

I finally charged to the front door to leave and saw that rain had, indeed, begun to fall just as I had predicted earlier in the afternoon. I mentally patted myself on the back for being right. I loved being right. My idea of hell was an eternity of always being wrong and having everybody else saying "I told you so" to me. I ran back to my office to get my Burberry off the coat rack. I shoved the .38 into the pocket, rushed back to the front door and picked up Anice to kiss her on the lips. I promised her I would be home at a reasonable hour and wondered how it would feel to leave home without having a guilt attack at not taking the dog with me. I tried not to look back at her little gray head and floppy ears looking out the window at me as I crossed the stepping stones and went out the wrought iron gate and onto the sidewalk.

I glanced up through the palm tree that hung over the walk from my front yard and saw low black clouds moving slowly across the sky. The only light came from the gas street lamp on the corner. Rain came down steadily and made the black pavement as shiny as the greasy hair of a silent screen star.

I got in the car and stepped on the starter button before turning the light switch on, reached up and turned on the windshield wiper, and wished they had put two wipers on this model instead of just the one on the driver's side. I eased the car carefully out onto the road and headed downtown to the hotel. By the time I had driven three blocks, I had the uneasy feeling that somebody was following me again. A set of headlamps behind me made at least two of the same turns that I did but I couldn't keep my eyes on him and the slick pavement at the same time so I took a quick turn through a rundown neighborhood and some back alleys trying to lose him and hoped for the best.

I found a pretty good parking place a half block

away and ran through the rain until I got under the balcony that stretched across the entire sidewalk for the length of the hotel. There were only a few people outside and my heart dropped to my feet from its previous position in my throat when I didn't see her. I hoped she might be waiting for me in the lobby and was headed that way when she stepped out of a shadow where she had been standing, looking in a shop window.

She turned and smiled when she saw me. My knees buckled, but I managed somehow to walk to her. She held her arms out shyly and I hugged her to me and said that I had missed her before I jumped back and looked nervously around to see if anybody was going to scream "Queer!" and begin tossing rocks at me. Nobody seemed to have even noticed us and the only person startled by my behavior was Lily. I grinned weakly and told her again how glad I was to see her.

Most of the people had gone into the hotel but a few latecomers rushed up the sidewalk toward the front doors. I wondered for a moment why they were in such a hurry, then remembered Benny Goodman. I looked at Lily and realized that Benny was very low on my list of priorities at that moment.

"Are you ready to go inside?" she asked, and smiled at me as though I were Greta Garbo, Eleanor Roosevelt, and Madame Curie rolled into one. I was the cat's pajamas.

We started to go into the hotel when I heard my name being called. I turned to the street and saw Gael and Katherine pulling up to the curb in Katherine's convertible. They were waving and Gael jumped out of the car. Her lip was curled in disgust.

"Katherine was worried about you and insisted we come up here. She nearly drove me crazy getting here."

"Worried about me? I'm fine. As a matter of fact, I've never been better." I laughed hysterically like a lunatic being goosed with a feather duster. I needed to get into bed and sleep for a week before men in white jackets came after me with a butterfly net.

"I don't know what got into her, but she was in a panic and kept saying she had a horrible feeling something was going to happen to you." She shrugged and rolled her eyes and grinned at us. "Y'all want to wait here while we park the car and we'll go listen to the band with you?"

"Sure. Lily, these are my friends, Gael and Katherine," I explained lamely as Gael headed back to where Katherine waited in her car. Lily looked puzzled but smiled graciously.

A group of people in evening clothes was coming toward us, one of them had fallen behind and was hurrying to catch up. He had on a plaid coat and a yellow fedora pulled down over his eyes but there was something vaguely familiar about him. I don't know if it was the way he held himself or what exactly brought him to my attention. I stared at him as the group, laughing excitedly at the prospect of their evening, drew closer. I realized suddenly that the man was not with the group at all and, as I watched, he reached under his coat and pulled out what seemed to be the longest gun I had ever seen. He aimed it in my general direction and in that instant I realized that the man was Cotton Peeples.

I reached in my pocket clawing for my pistol and heard Katherine screaming something to Gael. Gael ran back to where I was, grabbing my arm and shoving Lily and me out of his line of fire. The people in the group in front of Cotton realized that something was happening and scattered. My gun was out of my pocket and I was aiming when Cotton suddenly tossed his gun in the air and began to do a grotesque jitterbug. He looked absolutely ridiculous. I was embarrassed at his lack of rhythm and wished he had stuck to the minuet. His arms and legs flapped and waved in the air. It all took less than fifteen seconds, but it seemed to happen in slow motion. There was a loud drumbeat in the background that I finally realized was a machine gun. I added one and one and got two. Somebody had turned a Tommy gun on us.

Gael and I grabbed each other and Lily and spread ourselves like peanut butter on the side of the building as the horrible drone of the gun seemed to go on for an eternity. Then it was over. Tires squealed and I jerked around to see a green sedan taking off down the street like a striped-assed ape. I could see the little black snout of the gun being pulled back inside the car, but I couldn't see a license plate or tell anything about the occupants of the car.

I heard someone screaming "Goddamn! Jesus Christ!" and realized it was me. Katherine's car did a U-turn on two wheels a half block down the street. Her tires screamed as she flew back to where we stood. People were getting up off the sidewalk where they had thrown themselves. The only person hurt was Cotton and he was as dead as a post.

People were screaming in horror and vomiting. Cotton's blood mixed with the rain and became pink as it spread across the sidewalk like an overturned Singapore Sling. Gael ran to the car as Katherine pulled up.

"Get in the car!" Katherine screamed. Her face was as white and stiff as a priest's collar. I grabbed Lily, pulled her to the car, and shoved her into the back seat as Gael jumped into the front.

Katherine floorboarded it and we took off after the green car, which had quite a head start. We had turned south on Main Street before I even got the door closed behind me. There was no traffic at that time of night and we could see the taillights of the green car several blocks ahead. Katherine concentrated on the car in front of us and stomped the pedal. The Cadillac skidded on the wet pavement but she jerked the wheel and got it back under control. Gael reached under her seat and pulled out a sawed-off shotgun as casually as though she were pulling out a fresh pack of cigarettes. Hell, I thought she had just been kidding earlier about having one. She cracked the gun and checked it for shells, gave a satisfied grunt, and nodded. She calmly rolled down the window and climbed out of it so she was sitting on the door with her head and body outside and just her legs in the car. She yelled for Katherine to hurry up and catch the jerks.

I leaned back in my seat and pulled out my pistol. I felt like Wyatt Earp getting ready for the O.K. Corral.

We were gaining on the car when something

occurred to me. I leaned over the front seat and pulled Gael back inside the car. "What the hell are we doing? Those assholes have a machine gun!"

Gael looked at me, thought about it for a second, and then calmly said, "Stop the car."

Katherine kept driving as though she had not heard a word.

"Stop the goddamn car!" Gael yelled.

Katherine didn't let up on the accelerator and it finally occurred to me that she was in shock and couldn't comprehend anything we were saying. I leaned up and massaged her shoulders and whispered to her that everything was okay and she could stop now. I could feel the tension leaving her body as I kept whispering to her. I looked into the rearview mirror and saw tears streaming down her face.

She pulled the car into a filling station at the next corner. We all watched the taillights of the green car disappear through the rain before she turned off the engine.

Katherine turned to Gael and screamed, "Don't ever yell at me again!" and burst into huge sobs and clutched Gael to her. "I thought you were dead!" she stammered as she cried and tried to catch her breath.

Lily had my arm in a death grip. I was going to have to have it amputated if I didn't get blood to it soon, so I pried her fingers loose. She was terrified and her eyes looked at me with the blind panic of a rabbit caught in a spotlight. I picked up one of her hands and began rubbing it and talking to her. Her lips quivered and those wonderful black eyes filled with tears.

"Who was that man? Why did this happen?" She was on the verge of hysteria, which was good, since it kept me from tearing out of the car and running up and down the street with a case of the screaming meemies.

We sat in the car without saying anything for a while before I noticed a green neon sign a few doors down that flashed LIQUOR. I pointed it out to Gael and she got out of the car and went to get a bottle.

A friendly service station attendant in a clean green uniform came smiling out and asked if we needed help. He looked in the car, saw the shotgun on the seat, cleaned off the windshield, told us to stay as long as we liked, and walked backwards into the service station. He stood peering out the window at us.

"Jesus, I wish he would quit looking at us — I feel like Ma Barker!" Katherine said tiredly.

Gael came back with a bottle of brandy and we passed it around, still without talking.

So far it had not turned out to be what you might think of as the perfect date. I was wondering what to do to turn the evening around when Lily looked at me and said, "Is this what you meant when you said that something always comes up to prevent your seeing Benny Goodman?"

"Shouldn't we go somewhere where they serve this shit in glasses at tables?" Gael asked as she passed the bottle to me.

"I couldn't possibly go in anywhere," Katherine said, looking at herself in the rearview mirror. She reached for her purse and began digging for her compact. "I'm a mess."

"You think you look bad, you should have seen

the guy back at the hotel," Gael said, wiggling her eyebrows up and down like Groucho Marx.

"So, where do y'all want to go?" I asked, trying to think of a place that wasn't frequented by a bunch of big-gutted, drunken newspaper reporters standing around guffawing and clawing themselves.

"How about a place with some jazz?" Gael suggested.

"I'd rather go some place quiet. I've had about all the noise I can stand for one night," I said.

Katherine nodded in agreement, still looking in the rearview mirror, dabbing on powder and rouge, and added, "And dark."

Lily, who had been reserved around Gael and Katherine, said, "There's a nice place above one of the shops in the River Oaks shopping center that's dark and quiet."

We grabbed at the suggestion and Katherine pulled back out into the street.

"Why don't you run me by the hotel and let me pick up my car and Lily and I will follow y'all over there," I said.

"What about the police?" Lily asked. "Don't you think they'll be wanting to talk to us? After all, we were witnesses to the murder."

I shook my head. "I'd rather wear Brillo Pad panties than try to explain this to the police."

"Explain what to the police?"

Lily didn't know anything about what had been happening. I hadn't told her about it the night before because it was too crazy. If I met somebody for the first time and she started telling me that burglars had broken into her house for an address book to kill a policeman, I'd think she was slap out of her mind and I'd get the hell away as fast as I could go. And I was extremely hesitant to tell her now. Even though she had just witnessed Cotton Peeples' murder, the whole story was insane.

Gael grinned at me like a jackass. "Well, go on and tell her what you wouldn't be able to explain to the police now that you've almost been gunned down like a Chicago gangster."

"I'll wait till we get to the bar," I growled.

We pulled up beside my car and Lily and I hopped quickly into it. Seven police cars blocked the street in front of the Rice and an ambulance was pulling up as I eased out into the road. A crowd had gathered at the scene and my skin crawled at the eeriness of the red blinking lights bathing the people standing in the rain looking at the aftermath of violence. I shivered from the cold and damp and the fear that flowed through me as I turned the corner and shifted gears. Lily pulled the blanket off the back seat and tucked it around us as we rode in silence.

When we got to the bar, Gael and Katherine were waiting inside at a small table in a dark corner. The room was almost empty because of the bad weather, but the bar was warm and cozy.

"This was a good idea — coming here." Katherine smiled at Lily and patted her hand.

Lily smiled. "I'm glad you like it. There should be a piano player coming in soon and the bartender makes the best gin drinks in town."

A waiter took our orders and we chatted lightly until the drinks were served.

"When are you going to tell me who that man was?" Lily finally asked. "Why was he trying to kill you?"

I told her everything that had happened and she didn't look as though she thought I was a pathological liar. It helped that Gael and Katherine were there to verify it all.

"I don't understand why Mr. Peeples would want to kill you." She was so polite. I doubted if anybody had ever called Cotton "Mr. Peeples" before. Too bad he had to be killed for it to happen.

"I doubt if he did have any reason of his own to kill me. I imagine somebody hired him to do it. Don't ask me who that would be. I can think of a lot of people who might like to kill me, but I can't think of one of them that would use old Cotton to do it. He was such a loser. He screwed up everything he ever attempted. Including killing me."

"Hell," Gael said, "even if he had fired the gun, I don't think he'd have hit you the way he was aiming. Good drink!" She leaned back and sipped her martini.

"Well, it's the most exciting thing that has ever happened to me," Lily exclaimed. "I've been going to the Rice Terrace almost every Friday night for five years and nothing like this has ever happened before!"

We looked at her in astonishment.

"But who were those men in the green car?" Katherine pointed out. "Why were they trying to kill you? It seems like people are standing in line to get a shot at you. And how come they missed? Of course, I'm glad they did. Don't get me wrong, but it seems almost impossible that all three of you aren't dead."

"I don't think they were trying to kill us or they surely would have succeeded. I'm positive that same car's been following me all day and I don't have the foggiest idea who it is. I don't know what they want but apparently they don't want me dead yet."

"Maybe they want to torture you first. Make you suffer," Gael growled helpfully.

I could always depend on her to make me feel better. "I really hadn't thought about that angle. I'll be able to sleep much more soundly tonight."

"I think you should stay at our house," Katherine said authoritatively. "You may not be safe at your house."

"What the hell makes you think I'd be safe at your house, either?"

"Is it possible the same person who hired Cotton to kill you would kill him to shut him up?" Lily asked. "Surely there aren't that many people running around out there hiring people to kill each other."

"A lot more than you seem to realize. You should have been reading your own paper while I worked for you," I teased.

"I read every word you ever wrote." She smiled, batting her eyes.

Gael fired up a Camel and said, "The way I see it is somebody hired Cotton to kill Joe, then told him to kill you. It sounds like they're trying to keep something quiet. Then somebody else who wants to find out what you know, killed Cotton before he could kill you." She made tight geometric gestures with her hands and cigarette to outline her theory.

"I don't know anything for anybody to kill me over," I pointed out. "It doesn't make sense."

"Somebody thinks you do, whether you do or not."

I rubbed my forehead. "Let's don't talk about it any more. I'm beginning to get a headache."

Katherine looked at her watch and yawned. "It's way past my bedtime. Although I'm sure I won't be able to sleep a wink after all of this."

"I'm sure I won't either," Lily agreed.

Gael leered at me secretly and kicked me under the table. I kicked her back so hard she grunted. Katherine sensed something was going on and cut her eyes at us in warning. She had already become protective of Lily.

We said goodnight and hugged each other, then ran to the cars. The rain was really coming down by this time.

"Would you like to go to my place for a drink?" I asked, my voice cracking. My nerves were stretched so tight that if anybody so much as bumped into me slightly, I would hum like a violin.

"Wherever you would like to go."

I cranked the car and drove to my house, which was only a few blocks away. We ran to the door and stood under the striped awning while I unlocked the door. Anice was hopping up and down in excitement as we came into the house.

"Hi, Anice. Remember me?" Lily asked and scooped Anice up to hug. Anice squealed, pretending that Lily had pinched her. Lily laughed and called her a silly girl. She went to the couch and sat down with Anice in her lap while I turned on the heater in the fireplace and put away our coats. I went to the kitchen and fixed drinks, turned on the radio and gave Lily her drink. She was wearing red again tonight and was so beautiful she took my breath away.

Anice rolled over on her back in Lily's lap to expose herself and Lily massaged her chest and legs. Anice was mesmerized, her mouth open in a small O. She rolled her head slightly to see if I was watching. She had dipped her face in the gravy her dinner had made and her beard was gummy and in five or six little points like a star that bent in all directions. She was a disgrace and I told her so. She never even blinked an eye.

"I like it," Lily said in a complimentary tone as though Anice had deliberately fixed her beard like that. "It looks like an art form."

Anice rolled her head toward me again and would have stuck out her tongue and given me a raspberry if she'd been able to blow.

Lily put Anice gently down on the couch and scooted toward me, then leaned over and kissed me on the lips. I almost swooned and wondered what the hell had come over me. I felt like a fool.

"I would like to go into the bedroom," she said quietly.

I couldn't talk so I took her hand to lead her into the bedroom. I was shaking so hard I could hardly walk but she either didn't notice or was kind enough to pretend not to. Anice seemed completely at ease as she pranced along with us.

I opened the wooden blinds so we could see the rain. Huge white veins of lightning shot from east to west and back again through the pitch black sky, then the entire sky turned purple-white and blinked rapidly. Thunder cracked and roared and the rain pelted the windows. We made love to the music of the storm.

Anice jumped on and off the bed for attention, then finally sat on the foot of the bed with her back to us, staring off into space to make sure I knew her feelings were hurt.

I leaned over and made snorting noises and pretended to snap at her until she flung herself over backwards to let me tickle her stomach. Lily called her a pretty girl and kissed her in spite of her nasty little beard. Anice smiled and went to sleep, snoring loudly.

I woke up early the next morning with my left arm numb from being under Lily and my right leg practically twisted around my neck so Anice would have plenty of room. Fifteen years ago I could have slept standing on my head, knotted like a pretzel and still leapt out of bed like a gazelle. Those days were over. Now if I so much as lifted my fork the wrong way, I could give myself whiplash.

I eased out of bed and gimped into the bathroom to brush my teeth before Lily woke up. Anice pranced in behind me and made woo-wooing noises like a small train.

"Okay, okay, okay, okay," I said, and patted her on the head. "Let's go for a walk." I peeked into the bedroom as we went past and saw that Lily was still asleep.

We double-timed it around the block and rushed

back to the house for gingersnaps. Lily had awakened and put on my white terry cloth robe. She was in the kitchen digging around for a coffee pot and crossed the room to kiss me.

I watched as she made coffee. She didn't seem to mind that we ate cookies for breakfast. My opinion of her, which had already been high, kept growing in leaps and bounds.

"How are you this morning?" she asked as she reached over and tried to pat the cowlick down on the back of my head.

"I feel great!" It was the truth. I may have ached from a few stiff muscles and a little arthritis but it was the kind of ache you'd have if you'd been kicked by a bunch of butterflies all night. "How about you?"

"I feel wonderful!" she exclaimed. "I feel like the weight of the world's been lifted from my shoulders. You can't imagine the relief after all these years of feeling different from everyone else. I can't believe I never realized this about myself. How could I have ignored these feelings for all this time? I feel capable of being in love for the first time in my life."

If anyone else had said it to me, I would have shoved them out the door and locked it. She seemed to be staking a claim on me and it wasn't bothering me. I didn't feel smothered. I even liked it. I liked it a lot.

"I can't wait to tell everybody!" she continued.

"Whoa! Hold it, Lily. What do you mean — tell everyone?"

"My friends. My parents. Andrew. They'll all be so happy for me."

"I think you're wrong. I know exactly how you feel. But none of those people will."

"No, you're wrong. You don't know them. Andrew will be relieved that it's not his fault I don't love him. Don't you see? He'll finally understand that it doesn't have a thing to do with him!"

"Andrew is a very unusual man if he's relieved to find out that his wife likes other women."

"Andrew and I are really nothing more than friends. He'll understand. And he will be free to be with whomever it is that he's seeing."

"Lily, trust me. Nobody you know is going to be happy that you like women. They not only won't like it, but they'll try to convince you not to see me again. The pressure they put on you will be tremendous."

She smiled. "You're so intense. There's nothing to be afraid of. My mother raised me with the idea that men are inferior — it was a little secret that women kept among themselves. Sex was an obligation — an awful obligation. I see now what she wanted for me. She'll be happy. Don't worry."

"Your mother may have wanted you to hate men, but I doubt seriously if she had this alternative in mind. She probably wanted you to be married and miserable. Or she may have intended for you to be alone — never be with anyone."

Lily frowned slightly. "I don't understand why this is so taboo. It's so natural."

"Let's change the subject," I said. "I didn't mean to upset you. Do whatever you feel comfortable with and don't let me or anyone else tell you how to live your life." I rubbed my forefinger gently across her forehead to brush away the frown. She closed her eyes and smiled.

We talked and laughed and drank more coffee

and ate cookies until she said she needed to go home to start her day.

I took a shower and got dressed and called Gael to make sure she was up and rolling.

"Hello, Calamity? This is Buffalo Bill. You ready to ride shotgun today? The mail must go through."

"Where are we going?" she grumped.

"To the airport to pick up Tony Mahan coming in from Los Angeles. Then we'll decide."

Lily was looking around the living room when I came back in. "I like your apartment. You've got some very interesting things."

The operative word here was interesting. She was probably talking about the round display cabinet with wings or maybe the floor lamp/ashtray with the built-in cigarette lighter that looked like a microphone. Not the same stuff you'd find in her house.

"I'm glad you like it. Maybe you'll come back again."

"As often as you'll have me."

My heart jumped like a B-girl at a convention.

Anice was waiting at the front door with her right ear stuck out at a right angle. This was a question mark in her vocabulary.

"All right. You can come."

She darted out the front door and out into the yard, carefully wading through every mud hole she could find. I scooped her up and wiped her off with the emergency towel before putting her in the car. She jumped onto Lily's lap and sat down.

I cranked the car and headed toward River Oaks. The rain was like a poor cousin who had come to visit for a few days and had moved in to live forever. The sky was a mass of dark pewter clouds that wept at the foolishness of man. Occasional lightning struck blows for reform, and thunder bellowed Repent! I rolled my eyes and smirked. Take sin away and I wouldn't have a damn thing to write about.

"Would you like to come to the house for dinner tonight?" Lily asked. "Anice could meet my dog, Ted."

"I didn't know you had a dog."

"Oh, yes. A Lhasa Apso."

"I've never heard of it," I said.

"They're from Tibet. The Dalai Lama sent a pair of them to a friend of mine in England. Ted is an offspring.

Anice rolled her eyes and sneered.

I said, "I think I would be more comfortable going out to eat at a restaurant, if you don't mind."

"All right. Be careful today. And if you see that green car again, go to the police."

I dropped her off at her front door and told her I would call as soon as I got back home that afternoon. Anice stood in the seat on her hind legs, staring out the window at Lily as we drove off.

When we got to Gael's, Anice menaced Jinx and ate her food while I drank all of the coffee in the pot and flirted with Katherine.

"I don't know why I let you and that dog in my house," Gael muttered as we settled in the car and headed to the airport.

I wiggled the car to Almeda Road down streets that weren't covered with water from the rain, turned east on Old Spanish Trail, took the Griggs

Road fork and turned south on Telephone Road. The fields near the airport were empty at this time of year except for dried-up Johnson grass and mud and sticks from dead cotton stalks that had been disked under last fall after the cotton had been picked. It was a dreary, depressing, low-income neighborhood with pawn shops, peep shows, nasty little cafes, and tough-looking rednecks.

As we neared the airport a DC-3, propellers screaming, flew overhead, going in for a landing on the muddy airstrip. I held my breath watching it bounce and skid. Gael held her cigarette halfway to her lips, her glittering eyes willing the plane to safety. We both exhaled and relaxed when it rolled to a stop.

I parked the car across the street from the front door of the Houston Municipal Airport, a two-story white cement building with vertical stripes of rounded peach-colored cement at wide intervals. The front doors were chrome and glass, an Egyptian god in cement relief standing guard over them, looking straight ahead, his arms in the air, the matter-of-fact expression on his face telling the world that it was perfectly normal for him to be watching over an airport in Houston, Texas, in nothing but a headdress and loincloth. I had certainly seen stranger things walking down the streets of Montrose on a Saturday night, and I was just glad they hadn't stuck an armadillo up there.

A small angular control tower of green glass perched on the top of the building with a ladder leading to it from the second floor. A man wearing a set of headphones sat in front of a big board with lights all over it talking into a mike. Men in black and yellow slickers ran around on the rain-soaked field with flags and flashlights. They gestured and flagged and flapped importantly.

We sat in the car for a few minutes waiting for the rain to let up a bit, then loped across the street into the building. My shoes were soaked and I felt like I'd wrapped my feet in chitlins. My pants were wet and clung to my calves. The temperature was cold enough to make me good and miserable.

We went to the American Airlines counter to find out if Tony's flight was on time. The agent was a friend of mine. John was tall and thin with deepset black eyes and receding hairline.

He put aside the thick book he had been reading, batted his eyes and smiled sweetly. "What are you doing out here?" he asked in a soft voice that sounded like a couple of magnolia trees mating during a full moon in front of a honeysuckle vine.

"Came to pick somebody up. What you reading there, John?" I asked, nodding toward the book.

He reached over and fondled it tenderly. "*Gone With The Wind.*" He whispered it in a reverent tone.

"Never heard of it," I barked and waved a hand to see how riled I could get him. It worked.

His eyebrows shot up into his hairline. His lips flattened until they looked like two razor blades. "Why you horrible heathen," he hissed. "How dare you use that tone of voice when speaking of the greatest story ever told about the South."

Gael looked worried and glanced around the room. "Cut it out, you two."

John and I laughed.

"Don't you know when somebody's pulling your leg?" John asked. "Hollis and I have to have a cat fight to get warmed up."

"I've heard of that book," Gael said. "Just came out, didn't it?"

"Yes." John smiled angelically. "I sleep with it and the Bible on the table beside my bed. I'm thinking about changing my name to Scarlett."

"That's all we need," I said, flaring my nostrils. "I guess you'll be wearing a hoop skirt to work."

"Buh!" He said indignantly and tossed his head. "Do you really have business out here or did you just come out here to bother me?"

"I'm meeting a flight from Los Angeles. Do you know if it's on time?"

"It just landed if you're talking about the ten forty-five."

Gael and I wandered over to look out the glass wall that was the back of the building. A man had pushed some steps over to the plane and the door slammed open for passengers to disembark. We laughed when the wind blew a stewardess' skirt up over her head as she climbed down the stairs. The passengers ran toward the building over makeshift wooden planking the airport personnel had put out for sidewalks to help with the mud. Men pulled their hats low to avoid the rain and women held umbrellas and newspapers over their heads. One man strolled along calmly, ignoring the wind and rain as though he was too important to be rained on. I stared closely at him as he crossed the field, sophisticated and worldly. His clothes didn't seem to be getting as wet as everyone else's; he seemed unaffected by anything the world or the heavens could throw at him. He was above it all.

"Shit! Would you look at that!" I whispered, pointing him out to Gael. But she was already looking at him.

"Who is that? Do you know him?"

"Andrew Delacroix."

She turned quickly and stared again out the window.

"Thinks pretty highly of himself, doesn't he? I thought you said he'd be in New York at least two more weeks."

"He was supposed to be. I wonder what the hell he's doing back here. And more importantly, what's he doing on a plane coming in from Los Angeles?"

I saw Tony crossing the airfield, pointed him out to Gael and told her to round him and his luggage up while I went back and talked to John.

He was reading his book as I approached. "What is it now, Hollis?" He sighed at the interruption.

"You see that man over there? The one just coming into the building?"

"Mr. Delacroix?"

"You know him?"

"Sure. He's out here at least twice a month."

"Do you know why he's coming in from Los Angeles when he's supposed to be in New York? I mean, is there any way he could have ended up on that flight if he's coming in from New York?"

"He's not coming in from New York. He went to South America. I wonder why he's back so soon. He usually stays a couple of weeks," John said speculatively. "He's barely had time to get down there and turn around. Maybe he changed his mind when he got there and had to come back by way of Mexico City and Los Angeles."

"Does he always go to South America?"

"No. Sometimes he goes to Washington, but mostly he goes to South America."

"D.C.?"

He nodded.

"Are you sure, John? This is important."

"Yes, I'm sure." His eyebrows rose with the tone of his voice.

"Where does he go in South America?"

"I don't remember. What's this all about, Hollis?"

"I don't know. Could you look at your books and see where he goes?"

"I can't. I could get fired for giving out information about passengers."

Gael had come up and was listening to the conversation. Tony was standing behind her.

"Hollis is having an affair with his wife and he found out and won't give her a divorce. This could be what she needs to go to court," Gael confided.

I looked at her, wondering if she had suddenly taken leave of her senses. She kicked me in the shins and wiggled her eyebrows craftily when John looked away.

"Well, why didn't you say so?" he said with his hands on his hips, and prissed off to check the logs on the counter behind him.

"Jesus Christ!" I hissed. "Why don't you just get on the loudspeaker and announce it to the entire airport? And what was all that shit about a divorce?" I stomped her foot to get even for the shin-kicking. Tony was watching us with suspicion. I turned to him. "Hi, Tony. This'll just take a minute."

John glided back to where we stood and clamped his lips shut and whispered out of the corner of his mouth, "Bolivia."

"Bolivia?" I asked, confused. "B-o-l-i-v-i-a." I spelled it out hoping an answer would be conjured up.

"That's what I said," he muttered, still talking out of the side of his mouth. "I hope this will help with the divorce."

Gael shrugged. "She's very rich and he doesn't want to let go of all of that money. He told her he'd give her the divorce if she'd give him half of everything she owns. Including the dog."

"Half of the dog? Why, I'd just turn around and take a great big old dump in his hand and tell him 'That's all of Tara you'll ever get!' " John shrieked in outrage.

I didn't know what the hell he was talking about, so I just thanked him. The rain was pounding down again as we ran to the car and hopped in. Anice wagged her nub excitedly and bit my nose. I sat looking out the window toward the airport doors.

"Well? Anytime between now and Christmas! What are we waiting on?" Gael said irritably.

"I want to see what he does when he comes out."

"Well, he'll probably do what everybody else does — stand between us and the sun and glow like a goddamn rainbow. What the hell difference does it make what he does?" She got surly if she went for more than a half hour without a cup of coffee and a cigarette.

"Why don't you smoke a goddamn cigarette and shut up?" I snarled and slouched down in my seat so just my eyes showed over the windowsill.

"What are you doing now? You look like a dwarf driving a car. If you're trying to be inconspicuous, it's not working."

I flapped my hand for her to be quiet. She dragged out a Camel and lit it.

A black limousine pulled up to the curb and Andrew Delacroix crossed elegantly to it. He not only was rich, he looked rich — and privileged. He was tall and stood straight with a military-like bearing although he had never been in the Army as far as I knew. The car swept importantly off with a swish of tires on wet pavement.

"That's a government car," Gael observed through the cloud of blue smoke that enveloped her head.

I watched the car pulling away and saw by the license plate that she was right. I hated it when somebody saw something I'd missed. For a moment I thought about acting like I didn't think it was important so she wouldn't rub it in for the next five thousand eons.

"You're right. I completely missed that. It's a good thing you're here," I said enthusiastically so that everyone would have to think I was a good loser. Gael eyed me distrustfully.

As we rode toward town, Tony asked me about Joe's death. I spared him the gory details and told him nothing about Colette Chateau, the apartment at the Plaza, or the possibility of Joe having been on the take.

At Earthman's Funeral Home, Gael and I sat in the hard chairs in the somber, dimly lit waiting room while Tony went in to be alone with the closed casket, which was draped with white flowers and surrounded by lighted candles. The funeral director was a pale man who looked like one of those fish that have lived in underground caves until they have evolved into blind albinos. His expression was one of dignified solemnity. I wanted to slap him on general principles.

"Are you family of the deceased? We would like to express our condolences." His smile was as stingy as dinner at the orphanage, his voice pompous.

Gael carefully blew smoke into his face and said quietly without moving her lips, "We don't want your condolences. The way we see it, you make your money off people dying so you couldn't be that sorry when somebody kicks the bucket. Am I right?"

He sputtered angrily and turned on his heel. I was glad Gael had been on hand to handle the situation. I couldn't do everything that had to be done.

Tony came red-eyed into the waiting room and we left the funeral home.

"Are y'all hungry?" I asked when we got back in the car. They all either said yes or wagged their tails.

"Where would you like to eat, Tony? You're the one who just spent fifteen hours on a plane."

"I'd like a hot dog from James' Cony Island. My Dad and I used to go there on Saturdays."

"Well, I think that's just fine." I smiled broadly at Gael, who winced. "Don't you think that's nice, Gael? Gael loves hot dogs."

I drove over to the restaurant on Walker Street where I got a couple of cheese Coneys for myself and one without onions for Anice. I can't stand a dog with onion breath. The big blonde waitress called us Hon as she spooned chili onto the hot dogs.

We ate our lunch and Gael made a meager attempt not to look like she was eating frog vomit. Back in the car Anice ate hers with the same expression Gael had worn. She took her time eating it but finally finished, climbed in my lap and burped in my face.

We took Tony to the Milby Hotel and got him settled in one of their medium-priced rooms for a dollar and a half a day. It wasn't as fancy as some of the hotels, but it was steam-heated and there were ceiling fans in the rooms. I told him if he needed anything to call me, otherwise I would pick him up for the funeral the next day.

I drove over to the Cotton Exchange Building on Prairie, and Gael and I went in for a drink at the Cotton Club. Some of the reporters that I had worked with usually dropped in there at lunch time for a drink or two or three.

I found the man I needed sitting in a booth in the back of the bar. His name was Steve Bonner. He was a quiet, intelligent man who played the trumpet with a jazz band on the weekends and reported world news on weekdays. I introduced him to Gael and ordered a round of drinks. I oiled Steve with a snifter of Napoleon.

"I need some information," I said after we had made a little small talk.

He pushed his glasses up onto the bridge of his nose and smiled gently. "What about?"

"Bolivia."

"Bolivia? Bolivia's a big subject. You'll have to be more specific than that."

"Recent history. Like within the last six months. For instance, why would a rich man be sneaking off down there and keeping it a secret from everybody."

"Hell, it could be anything from a mistress to fucking a donkey. You know that."

"I don't think that's it. He doesn't look like a donkey fucker to me and, believe me, I've known my share. How about drugs, gambling, something of that nature?"

"Possible. But most drugs come from Columbia. And most people go to Rio to gamble."

"I think the man is up to something illegal and the odd thing is that a government car met him at the airport."

"You think that's odd with all the crooks we have in Washington?" Steve asked, astounded.

"Could you just do a little checking around for me? See if something jumps out and grabs your eye."

"Sure. If I get a chance, I'll do it this afternoon."

I stood up and paid the waiter. "Thanks again, Cheese."

We went back to the car and I had to wake Anice from her nap in the driver's seat. She glared grumpily at me and flounced over to sit in Gael's lap.

The fresh air smelled good after being in the stuffy bar and the rain felt cool on my face.

"Where to?" Gael asked.

"Home. I was thinking about dropping by the Plaza and rattling Colette's cage to see what kind of shit fell out, but I think that can wait. I need to make a couple of phone calls and maybe squeak a nap in before I call Lily. I doubt seriously if we'll be having dinner since her husband came home, though."

I dropped Gael off at her house and hoped she didn't notice the green car behind me a couple of blocks when I drove off.

I was tired of worrying about the green car. I drove straight home, got out of my car and stood beside it holding Anice. I could see the other car parked down Woodhead on the other side of Westheimer a couple of blocks away. I wiggled my fingers at them in a friendly wave. If they mowed me down, they just mowed me down. There wasn't a goddamn thing I could do about it. I couldn't make out the license plate number from where I stood or tell anything about the occupants of the car, which looked like a '34 Chevrolet.

I opened the wrought iron gate to my front yard and went into the house thinking that I should probably head straight out the back door and work my way around behind the green car by cutting through the dry cleaners on Westheimer and going through some back yards to Harold Street. I might at least be able to get the license plate number. I figured the car was stolen, or, at the very least, the plates were, but you never know. I went into my office and grabbed my binoculars and was heading for the back door when the phone rang.

It was Lily. "Hello, my darling."

She was the only person I had ever heard use that expression of endearment and have it sound natural. "Hi. I'm glad you called. I just walked in the door. How are you?"

"You aren't going to believe this, but Andrew came home unexpectedly. He's here now."

"He's in the room with you?"

"No. He's downstairs. I told him everything."

"No!"

"Yes, and he reacted just as I told you he would. He's very happy for me."

"No!"

"Yes. And he wants you to come for dinner tonight so he can tell you so himself."

"No!"

"Does that mean no, as an expression of disbelief and wonder, or no, you won't come to dinner?"

"I'm not sure what it means. This is all going a little too fast for me, Lily. I don't mean you and me, I mean this stuff with Andrew."

It went against everything I knew about human nature for him to be happy for Lily. Even if he wasn't in love with her, he wouldn't want her to be having an affair. It's not normal to leap with joy when you find out your spouse has found someone new — especially if that someone is of the same sex.

People who don't react in a normal manner make me nervous. There was nothing I had seen about Andrew Delacroix so far to indicate he was some kind of preternaturally unselfish, sweet, forgiving spirit who would be happy for his wife to find happiness elsewhere.

The man had thin lips, for Christ's sake. You look that much like a lizard, you probably are one. He might be able to fool Lily, but he couldn't fool me. It was my job and had been for a long time to see the seamy side of people. She, on the other hand, looked for the beauty in everything. When I saw something beautiful, I looked for the price tag.

"Please come to dinner," Lily pleaded. "It would mean so much to me. You'll like Andrew when you get to know him. I know you will."

I knew I wouldn't. I formed my opinion of people in the first five seconds of meeting them. I knew an asshole when I saw one, and Andrew Delacroix was a first class, grade-A, certified, card-carrying asshole.

"Lily," I said, "I really don't think it's a good idea."

The silence on the other end of the line told me I had hurt her. More than anything else in the world I didn't want to do that. I realized how much this meant to her, and how much she meant to me. Having dinner with her and her husband wouldn't be a pleasant experience — as a matter of fact, it would probably be downright nasty. But she didn't know that. She really thought everything was going to be hunky-dory. Oh, well, I figured I could put up with just about anything for a couple of hours if it would make her happy. Besides, it would give him the opportunity to show everyone exactly what kind of an asshole I knew he really was.

"How about if I come for drinks after dinner?" I compromised. That way he wouldn't get the chance to make a snide comment if I used the wrong fork or dribbled something on my shirt. I wasn't sophisticated enough to be comfortable sitting around yukking it up with a woman I was sleeping with and her husband.

I could tell she was slightly disappointed, but she said she understood and that drinks would be fine. I told her I'd be there at about nine o'clock.

"I've missed you today," she added in her husky voice that was sexy and sweet at the same time, the kind of voice that made you feel like Irene Dunne was in your kitchen in a negligee baking an apple pie.

"I missed you, too," I said. "I'll be glad to see you tonight."

She hung up and I waited, holding on just in case. Just as I suspected, there was a second click a few seconds later from another receiver being put down.

I hung up with a sense of dread. I felt like I was going to an ice skating party in roller skates and my birthday suit.

There wasn't a goddamn thing I could do but take a nap, so I did. I was just waking up when the phone rang again.

This time it was Frank Brumfield.

"A bum named Cotton Peeples was iced in front of the Rice Hotel last night. A car full of torpedoes sprayed the front of the building with a machine gun. Of course, it may have just been some elaborate advertisement by Warner Brothers Studio for the latest James Cagney movie, but we down here at the police station tend to think not. But, of course, that is just our humble opinion."

"And a very pleasant good afternoon to you, too, Lieutenant. I'm just fine, thank you. And you?" I yawned, trying to wake up enough to see the clock on my dresser.

"Cut the shit, Hollis. Eyewitnesses said somebody who sounded suspiciously like you jumped into a big light-colored car and fled the scene. They also said that Cotton was aiming the weapon found by his body at the person who fits your description when he was gunned down."

"Did they say that that person was extremely good-looking?"

"No, they didn't say that." He sighed deeply.

"Well, there you have it. They couldn't possibly have been talking about me."

"I think it's about time for you to mosey on down here again so we can have another one of our little tête-à-têtes, Hollis. It makes me mighty suspicious when you find a police officer dead then some third-rate bum tries to gun you down a few days later. Especially when that third-rate bum works for the same paper you do."

"What are you talking about?"

"Are you trying to tell me you didn't know that?"

"I don't know everybody that works for the *Times*. Besides, I don't work there anymore. I quit. Kaput. No more."

"That makes it even more interesting."

"Why? Do you think they send a hit man to gun down all former employees? Keep them from going to work for the competition."

"Why are you such a goddamned smart-ass?"

I assumed it was a rhetorical question and that he didn't really want an answer.

"He worked in the circulation department until a few weeks ago when he quit showing up. Of course, I'm just a dumb, ignorant cop who doesn't know my butt from third base, but I think it's more than coincidence."

"What do you think, Frank? I had him killed for not getting my paper delivered on time?"

"If you don't cut the wisecracking and level with me, I'm going to have you picked up. I'm sick and tired of dealing with smart-asses."

"Well, I'm sick and tired of dealing with a bunch of rude sons of bitching cops. Where'd y'all learn your manners — at a dog fight? I don't know who killed Joe or Cotton Peeples. If I did, I'd probably tell you if you said please. Unfortunately, I don't know anything. I don't like finding people dead and I don't like people shooting at me. And I don't like cops bullying me, and I don't like it that one more time I didn't get to see Benny Goodman. I don't like a lot of things and I know even less than I like."

"Why didn't you stick around the hotel last night?"

"Because I tried to chase down the car full of torpedoes but I couldn't catch them."

"Why didn't you come back to the scene?"

"Because I didn't know anything and I knew that cops being what they are, they wouldn't believe me and I'd be having a bunch of meaningless conversations like this one. And because I'm tired of looking at corpses lying around bleeding all over everything. Call me flighty and irresponsible, but there it is. I've had to do enough of that with my job to not want to do it while I'm out for a night on the town. I know that must be hard for you to understand but that's just the kind of girl I am."

"Are you sure you didn't know Cotton from work?"

"Yes."

"Do you know who killed him?"

"No."

"Do you know anything that would help at all?"

"No, but if you'll hum a few bars, I'll try to play it by ear. Haven't you been listening to a goddamn thing I've said?"

"Just don't leave town without letting me know," he grated.

"Well, that's too bad. I was planning my annual trip to Holland to sniff the tulips next week. I guess I'll have to put my wooden shoes back on the shelf."

"I'm warning you." He slammed the phone down.

I grinned to myself. I always felt invigorated after a round or two with the cops. It sharpened my wits. Kept me on my toes. Besides, I liked Frank.

I chuckled to myself. He hadn't gotten any information out of me, but I had gotten some out of him. I had not told him that the mugs that had mowed down Cotton were parked a mere two blocks from my house and were probably just waiting for the perfect opportunity to drill me as full of holes as a pair of wingtip shoes. That was a hot one. I laughed and laughed and laughed. I was clever all right. I wondered why I hadn't told him. Maybe I had just gotten used to dragging the bums around behind me like an extra set of buttocks.

I called for Steve Bonner at the *Times.* Greg Benson, who shared a partner's desk with Steve, picked up his phone.

"Steve had to go over to the courthouse for something or other," he told me. "He said if you called to tell you to call back. He has something for you."

"Did he say what it was?"

"No. But he sounded kind of excited."

I thanked Greg and hung up. I hated to wait. Patience was not one of my virtues. I shuffled off to the bathroom and took a long hot bubble bath with my dark glasses on and my little sailboat that floats in the tub. I pretended I was in the Virgin Islands on a beach with a cool rum drink in my hand. I stayed on St. Thomas until I got tired of it then pushed the little boat around the tub. Bubbles soon became a dense fog around the Cape of Good Hope — a fierce storm developed and threatened the brave travelers going to the strange new world. I kicked a wave up with my foot. Crash! It battered against the boat. I kicked up another wave that engulfed the boat. It sank. Oh well, they couldn't all make it to the New World.

I was considering salvaging the boat when my phone rang.

I ignored it and stuck my big toe up into the faucet and stared at it for a while thinking that if the call was important, whoever it was would call back. The phone quit after fourteen rings.

It was time to get out of the tub before my skin wrinkled permanently. I ambled into the bedroom and saw that it was only four o'clock. I didn't want to get dressed that early and have my clothes get all wrinkled before I got to Lily's.

The phone rang again.

"Ma Bell," I said into the mouthpiece as I lay down on the bed.

"Is this Hollis Carpenter?" a whiny cheap voice asked. I could practically smell the Evening In Paris through the telephone.

"Yes."

"This is Colette. You remember me?"

"Yes." I took a deep breath and held it with my cheeks puffed out. Then exhaled.

"I have some information I think you'll be interested in." She said it inta-rested with the accent on rest.

"Okay. Go ahead."

"It ain't free."

"Well, that figures. What kind of information is it?"

"You said you wanted to know how Joe got his money, dincha? Well, I know. If you wanna know, you gotta pay."

"How much?"

"Two hunnerd dollars."

"Two hundred dollars?" I repeated, partly so I could scream with outrage and partly so I could pronounce "hundred" correctly. "You could almost buy a new car for two hundred!" I wondered if syphilis had eaten her brain up.

"Look. I just called up Joe's lawyer and found out the son of a bitch left everything including that dump of a house to the kid. He didn't leave me one red cent. So I'm stuck in this hell hole of a town without a dime. I'm ready to blow this joint and head out to California — maybe Hollywood. See about a acting career. I shoulda been a actor. Everybody back home said so. I got good cheekbones."

"I don't have two hundred dollars."

"Get it from your paper. They'll pay for a big story."

"I don't work for the paper anymore."

"So, Miss High and Mighty reporter done got herself fired. What the hell, you can sell it to another paper, I bet. If you want the scoop, you'll get the money. You want it or not?"

"Maybe. But you'll have to give me more information than that. You may think the story is important but it may not be worth a plug nickel."

"Oh, it's worth it, all right."

I could tell by her voice that it probably was worth it. Or at least she thought it was. I tried to fish more out of her, but she wasn't having any part of it.

"Look, Miss Chateau. I might be able to borrow some money, but I'll have to know more than you've given me. I can't just borrow money on your word."

"On my word!" she shrieked. "You act like I'm scum or something! You can't treat me like that, you bitch."

"Calm down. I couldn't borrow that kind of money on Abraham Lincoln's word with so little information."

She sniveled and blew her nose so loudly I had to hold the receiver away from my ear. "It's about those guns disappearing. But that's all I'm going to tell you." She eked the information out like an orphan sharing candy.

Oh, hell. Those guns again. I hadn't wanted any part of that story from the first. I hadn't thought there was much of a story there. Evidence disappeared all the time. I figured whoever had owned the guns in the first place had probably bribed some cop to get them back for him. Or maybe some other mob boss wanted them cheap. Who knows. Maybe I'd had some kind of intuition that I would find out something I didn't want to know.

"Okay. Let me see what I can do. I'll have to make a few phone calls to see if I can get the money. I doubt if I can get two hundred, but I'll see what I can do. Maybe fifty — a hundred tops."

"You want this info, you show up here with two hunnerd dollars."

"Are you going to be home for the rest of the

evening? It may take a while. If I get it, I'll just drop by. And I don't want any surprises like Darryl Wade being there, either. If anybody else is there, I won't come in."

I knew it would surprise her and it did.

"What do you mean?"

"Come on, Colette. I know about you and Darryl. I know you were seeing him on the sly while Joe was alive. What's he going to do if you leave town? He might not like that at all." If I agitated her and got her on the defensive, she'd be more likely to take whatever amount of money I offered.

"Darryl don't give a shit what I do and I don't give a shit what he does, neither. He's a mean bastard and he can go find somebody else to beat on when I'm gone."

She was scared in spite of her words. She was good and scared. At least I knew why she was willing to talk all of a sudden. Darryl had probably started whipping up on her pretty good since Joe wasn't around to take care of her. What a life.

"Just hurry up and get here with the money, okay? When I tell you this shit, I gotta get on outta town."

"Let her stew in her own juices," I mumbled to myself and hung out in the closet awhile trying to decide what color pants to wear. I finally put on some gray ones and a black sweater and got my shoes from in front of the bathroom heater where I had put them to dry out. They were still gummy like a piece of rawhide after Anice has chewed it for a few hours.

I admired myself in the mirror for a couple of minutes, then went into the kitchen and opened the cookie jar where I kept my life savings. I pawed through the grubby bills under the dried-up cookies and pulled out a hundred dollars. I had lied to Colette. I had managed to stash away four hundred dollars to show for fifteen years of work but I was goddamned if I was going to give half of it to some hooker for information about how crooked the Houston Police Department was. I clutched the bills in my hand and kissed them goodbye. It hurt me physically — in this case, parting wasn't such sweet sorrow.

Anice wanted to go with me and I decided to take her since there was too much craziness going on right now to leave her at home alone. I picked her up and stuffed her inside my coat, which meant I couldn't button the top two buttons.

"We need to go on a diet, you little rat dog!" I said. She sneered. She was proud of her full figure.

I put the .38 in my coat pocket and went back for the .25, which I stuffed in the waist band of my pants under the sweater. If I'd had a bazooka, I'd have taken that, too. I was scared. Something was fixing to happen, I could feel it in my bones. I had on my lucky red underwear and my diamond earring. I tried to think if I had any other good luck dinguses to take along.

I headed the car south down Woodhead. The green car was gone. I thought about going to Gael's and getting her to ride along, but decided she had done enough to help. She couldn't play nursemaid forever.

An hour had passed from the time I had hung up from Colette until I parked on Montrose

Boulevard in front of the Plaza Hotel. I grabbed the blanket out of the back seat and covered Anice so she would be warm while I was inside. I gave her one of the emergency gingersnaps from the coat pocket that didn't have a gun in it and went into the hotel.

The desk clerk was nowhere to be seen. The sound of a man's voice singing the blues accompanied by a piano floated out of the bar. I stood with my eyes closed and let the sound move through me. Some of my tension lifted and I smiled at myself for having the heebie jeebies. I took a deep breath and held it to release more of the tension. I hadn't realized what a case of the creeps I had developed. It was time to take a vacation before I started seeing creatures with bloody fangs and hair on their knuckles howling at the moon.

I went to the elevator, nodding in time to the music and decided to stop in the bar on the way out and listen awhile.

On the fourth floor, I stepped jauntily out into the hallway which was completely empty — except for the crowd of about thirty people standing in a knot on their tiptoes craning to see over each other's heads in front of Colette Chateau's door.

Cold sweat broke out all over my body. I could have just gotten back on the elevator without even asking. Instead, I walked down the hall. My legs were made of lead and the hallway kept getting longer and longer. I walked for well over a hundred and forty-five years, but I finally made it. An old lady in a black wool dress, her silver hair braided and wrapped around her head like a crown, stood at the very back of the crowd. I tapped her on the shoulder and asked what had happened, although I really didn't want to hear it.

"Girl's been killed in there. Head smashed in. Somebody said she was a woman of ill repute, but I don't care. She still didn't deserve to die."

"Christ on a crutch," I muttered. My heart raced erratically like a peglegged sprinter. My body shook convulsively. "Did anybody call the police yet?"

"Mr. Barham called from his apartment across the hall." She pointed at an apartment door and we both turned and stared at it in awe. It's funny how in a murder case, everything that pertains to the people involved, no matter how insignificant, suddenly develops an importance that it never would have had otherwise.

"Did anybody see who did it?" I asked.

She shook her head. "I'm scared to death we've got a murderer stalking the halls. I'll probably call my daughter and go stay with her until they catch him. I'm certainly not going to stay here!" Her eyes glittered. You wouldn't have been able to blast her out of that hotel with a case of dynamite. It was a gruesome murder but it would give the residents something to talk about over coffee besides whether or not they'd been to the bathroom.

I could hear a siren in the distance so I ran back to the elevator and banged on the button. The doors seemed to creep open and the ride down was as slow as Jack Benny reaching for the check at a four-star restaurant.

In the lobby I headed for the phone booth. I sat down and waited, listening to the fan that came on when I closed the hinged door. Two cops stormed through the front doors into the lobby and rushed to the elevator. I dropped a nickel into the phone and dialed the police station.

"Frank Brumfield, please." My voice was ragged and I breathed deeply a few times while I was waiting for him to answer.

"Brumfield."

"Frank. It's Hollis. Is Darryl Wade there?"

"No, he's not and I don't have time for you right now."

"I know that. You're on your way to the Plaza Hotel to investigate the murder of a prostitute."

"How did you know that?" His voice got low and mean.

"I'm here. At the Plaza."

"What are you doing there?"

"She called me about an hour ago wanting money to leave town. By the time I got here, a crowd was outside her door. She was already dead."

"Well, now. How many does that make? Joe, Cotton Peeples, and now this whore. What are you? Typhoid Mary? I can't ignore this any longer, Hollis. You wait where you are until I get there."

"Don't be a goddamned fool, Frank. You've always had more sense than that. Most cops couldn't shoot themselves in the ass with a twelve-gauge shotgun if somebody else aimed it for 'em. Don't go stupid on me."

"Stay at the Plaza, Hollis."

"No, Frank. You can't tell me what to do. You want to arrest me, get a warrant and do it. I'll be at my house later on tonight. In the meantime, you'll be giving the murderer time to destroy evidence you could use to pin him to the wall. Hell, he may even get completely away if you're that dumb."

"Don't goddammit call me dumb! I've had it up to here with you! You're so goddamned smart. Who did it? As far as I'm concerned, you look just about as good for it as anybody else.

"Aw, shove it up your ass, Frank. I've a good mind not to solve any more cases for you. See how many little old ladies you bring in for violent crimes instead of the real criminal. There's one upstairs you could nab for this one. Be careful if you go after her, she looks like she could put up a hell of a fight with a couple of bobby pins and —"

"Shut up!" he screamed. The man was going to have a heart attack if he didn't learn how to take it as well as dish it out. "You know who did it?"

"Sure I know who did it. Don't you?" I couldn't stop myself from needling him. It was calming me down, though. The more agitated he became, the cooler I got.

"If you have any information, give it to me."

"Say please."

"You'll think please when I have you locked up so far down in the jail they have to pipe sunshine in to you."

"I guess that's as close as you can get to being polite, Frank. Darryl Wade did it, as if you didn't know."

"Darryl Wade!"

"Yeah, Frank. Darryl Wade."

"Why would he do a thing like that?"

"Come on. You knew damn well he was having a fling with her. She was Joe's girlfriend and she was chipping on him with Darryl. For all I know, he killed Joe, too, to get him out of the way. Maybe he got tired of sharing her with Joe."

"You don't really expect me to believe this bullshit, do you?" he snarled.

"Yes, I do. And if you hurry, you might catch him with the clothes he had on when he killed her. There's bound to be blood or makeup or perfume or something on them. But if you insist on wasting time on me, he'll burn them or throw them in the ship channel. Besides, you know goddamned well I didn't have anything to do with those murders, Frank. So, adios, old friend."

I slammed the phone down as hard as I could and ambled casually out to my car. Three other police cars had come up while I was on the phone and the officers were busy cordoning off the front of the hotel. Anice climbed importantly into my lap and barked at the policemen as I pulled away from the curb. I tried to smile calmly and not look guilty, which is hard for me to do. My heart pounded and I couldn't catch my breath. I sent up a silent prayer that Frank hadn't been able to get to the radio and put it on the air for them to detain me.

I was just pulling away when an officer yelled and ran after me. Oh shit! He ran up beside the car. I rolled the window down and smiled politely. "Yes, officer?"

"What kind of dog is that? She sure is cute." He reached in to pat her on the head.

Please, God, don't let her bite him. "She's a Schnauzer. Most of them have ears that stick up but I didn't want to clip hers because of the pain. That's why hers are floppy," I babbled, unable to stop myself.

He grinned and patted her again. She wagged her nub and barked again. He laughed and waved us on. I ground the gears getting away.

I put a good distance between me and the Plaza before stopping at a Texaco filling station on Main Street to use the phone.

A grease monkey was under a rusted out T-model trying to put it back together with chewing gum and bailing wire. An old farmer in faded overalls and an old green army overcoat that he had probably worn in the Battle of the Argonne Forest, stood to one side watching.

I squatted down beside the car and peered under it at the mechanic. "Hi. I was wondering if I could use your phone, please."

"Sure. Help yourself, little lady."

I glanced around to see who he was talking to before I realized it was me. I thanked him and went into the office that smelled like old black grease and gasoline. A pain shot through my knee. I must have twisted it again in all the excitement.

The gas heater was lit in the office and the warmth felt good. It wasn't raining like it had been, but there was a fine mist and a cold fog was rolling in. You never knew what to expect from Houston weather. Hell, by tomorrow, we could all be out sunbathing.

I sat down in the golden oak swivel chair behind the plain dark oak desk. I took two Kleenex from a box on the desk to hold the phone so I wouldn't get grease all over myself.

I called Steve at the *Times* and caught him as he was leaving work for the evening. He had found out about two or three things going on in Bolivia that he thought were interesting. But only one of the items interested me and I knew now why Andrew Delacroix was going there. The fog in my head was lifting a little. I made a bet with myself that if I was wrong, I'd hang up my typewriter and start selling home permanents door to door in Dallas. I thanked Steve and reminded myself to pick him up a bottle of brandy sometime in the near future.

I leaned back in the chair and stared out the plate glass window of the filling station, trying to decide what to do next. There were disgusting little mounds of housefly corpses on the windowsill left over from summer. I rubbed my forehead and did some chin exercises, then finally hunched over the desk and picked up the phone again.

This time I called the police station and asked for the officer in charge of the evidence room. A weak-willed, pussy-whipped desk sergeant answered and I browbeat it out of him that the guns had disappeared from a warehouse on William Street. The police department had warehouses scattered around town in various locations to house evidence taken in raids on gangs and gambling halls and such. They stored slots and marble machines and whiskey stills and guns and even some stolen cars. They still had bootleg stored from prohibition days. I had read in the *Chronicle* two days before that deputy sheriffs were just now getting around to pouring out 'shookup gin' and pre-repeal corn stored in the basement of the courthouse. Shit was stored all over this town. Somebody had said they'd stored the car down here that Bonnie Parker and Clyde Barrow had been killed in two years before, but I think that was just a rumor started by some old drunk reporter opening his mouth to hear his gums flap. I got the exact location of the warehouse by lying to the sergeant that I was with the District Attorney's office.

I hung up and sat for a while in the warmth of the office, watching the fog outside getting thicker by the minute. I could barely see buildings two blocks away. My watch reminded me that darkness would be falling in about thirty minutes.

I still had a few hours to wait before I needed to be at Lily's house. Why the hell had I agreed to do that? I must have been out of my mind.

I got up, stretched, and remembered the car was low on gas. I filled it up myself instead of bothering the mechanic, and stood watching the glass bowl on top of the pump and staring hypnotized by the dials going around, totting up the bill. Seventeen cents a gallon — goddamn price-gouging oil companies.

I dug the money out of my pocket and went back to the garage and hollered at the mechanic that I would leave it inside on his desk. He yelled something back which I took to mean okay.

Anice stood in my lap, pawing at the window as we drove through downtown. I turned down an alley with a concrete gutter in the middle of it and eased around to the front of the warehouse. I had taken my time through town, watching the blinking, colorful signs. I hadn't been in a killing hurry to go to that area of town at that time of night — or at any time of night, for that matter. The streets were deserted, dark, dreary, and damp. I parked in front of the concrete steps that led up to the concrete loading dock that stretched across the front of the dark red brick building. Big roll-up doors were protected at night by iron gates that folded back during the day. The porch roof covering the loading dock was made of big oak beams and held up by four-by-four oak columns. A regular-sized wooden door that looked like it would withstand an Indian attack, if need be, stood in the center of the building. I took the flashlight out of the glove box and started up the steps of the building. I went back to the car and got Anice. I snapped her leash on and she stood importantly waiting for me to help her out of the car. She knew I needed her for protection. She was too little and pudgy to get up the steps by herself so I carried her up to the dock. I went to the front door and knocked. The building was so big and the door so thick that I might as well have been patting a down pillow with a flour tortilla. I banged on it with the butt of the flash to no avail. I tried the knob which wasn't locked, so I opened the door and went in.

The warehouse was huge and so dimly lit by a couple of sixty-watt light bulbs that they could have saved the electric bill by catching a dozen fireflies and sticking them in a jar and hanging them by a string from the ceiling. All the light did was create grotesque shadows for hideous scar-faced ax murderers to hide behind. I reached into my pocket to touch my pistol. It felt cold and hard and reassuring. A room off to the right in the far back corner had plate glass windows that began at chest level and went up to the ceiling. A dim naked yellow bulb hung from a cord in the center of the office. I headed in that direction.

"Hello!" I yelled so nobody would accidentally blow my head off.

Someone stood up in the office and ran his fingers through his short red and gray hair.

"Who is it?" he yelled back.

"It's Alice Toklas from the D.A.'s office," I yelled.

I went into the office, trying to look official and hoping he wouldn't think it was strange that someone from the D.A.'s office would bring a dog on official business. Anice pranced ahead, sniffed the rag rug on the floor, squatted, and wee'd to let the man know who was in charge of the situation. I sneered to let him know that bringing a dog to wee on the rug was a standard procedure for the D.A.

"Are you James Woods?" I asked.

"Yeah." He eyed me suspiciously and scratched his rear end. That seemed to help some men think more clearly — that or scratching their nuts. His eyes glazed over and he stared off into space, clawing slowly. "What do you want?"

"If you can get your fingers out of your rear end for a few minutes," I snarled, "I'd like to ask you some questions about those guns stolen from here about two weeks ago." Maybe they believe that they suddenly become invisible when they scratch. He had the decency to blush and quit digging.

"I thought y'all had closed that investigation."

"Well, you thought wrong." I figured the only way to bluff my way through was by acting as rudely as possible. "This whole thing stinks of dirty cop, and believe me, Officer Woods, our District Attorney is sick to death of dirty cops, in case you haven't read the newspaper lately. He's been shaking them by their privates like maracas."

He nodded. Sweat beads were breaking out on his forehead and upper lip. His tongue darted out nervously and ran across his lips a few times. He took a few steps backward until the back of his calves touched the iron cot in the corner where he had been napping when I first came into the warehouse. I could smell his fear across the room. It floated across to me on the whiskey fumes of his breath. His face was pale and bloated and his red nose stood out like mud thrown on the wall of a church sanctuary. He glanced rapidly from me to the pillow on his cot.

"Go ahead," I said. I knew I had him by the balls now. "Take a drink. I won't tell anybody. You look like you need one."

He was pathetic as he reached under the pillow and dragged out a bottle of what looked like sheep piss. And this was cow country. He gulped down a few swallows and shivered convulsively. His face looked like the booze tasted like shit, but he drank some more anyway.

"Now why don't you tell me all about the night the guns got stolen?"

His eyes darted around like a rat trapped by a terrier. He wiped his mouth with the back of his hand and pumped his chest out like a big shot. "Well, it happened about eight-thirty. I was laying here listening to the radio when all hell busted loose. These two fellers broke in here with shotguns and tied me face down to the cot. They told me if I tried to fight, they was going to shoot me. There wasn't nothing I could do about it. Then they went back out of the office and took the guns out."

"How many guns were there?"

"Bout a thousand."

"A thousand?" I shrieked before I could stop myself. The rumors that I'd heard had estimated anywhere from a hundred to a hundred and fifty. That was why I hadn't paid much attention to it. Who cared about a hundred or so guns? A thousand was a whole different ballgame. "It must have taken them all night to load them."

He shrugged, braver now. The sheep piss was kicking in.

I said, "They must have had some help loading them, and had to've had at least two pretty good sized trucks to haul them away."

"I dunno, mebbe. I couldn't see nothin. I was tied up the whole time," said the fountain of information. He was beginning to slur his words and his tone was surly. I wanted to slap the snot out of him. Figuratively, of course.

My mind was racing a thousand miles an hour. Ideas were banging into each other like drunks on a dance floor. How could that many guns disappear in Houston, Texas? It seemed like I would have heard by now who had gotten them or where they were stashed. I found it hard to believe that two whole weeks had passed and somebody hadn't blabbed like an old lady at a bingo game.

I went fishing. "Did you hear them say where they were taking them?"

He shook his head. His mouth was closed tightly and his hands gripped his knees.

"Maybe they were taking them up north

somewhere? Or maybe to Galveston?" I stabbed viciously in the dark.

He didn't respond.

"Are you sure you didn't hear anything?"

He sat there like a stump.

"Maybe they were shipped out of the country?" It was the only thing that made any sense. A bell rang in my head — I remembered Bill Oswald saying the same thing about a hundred years before. Bill always knew everything. He had already given me the answer. Why the hell hadn't I listened to him? I surely would have heard something by now if those guns were still in Houston. I had turned away from the drunk while I was thinking. When I looked back at him, he was bug-eyed. I was right. They had been shipped out of the country.

"All right, you don't know anything. Thanks for your time, anyhow," I said, grinning stupidly.

"Oh, sure. Anytime." His eyes were relieved and his mouth hung open as I went out the door. I strolled casually through the warehouse and out. I raced down the steps and put Anice in the car and rushed back up the steps. I could see Woods in the office on the phone flapping his arms wildly. I made my way stealthily back through the shadows to the office, praying he wouldn't turn and look out the window. I didn't need to worry about it. He was too busy being scared. I bent over double and scurried over to the office and squatted outside the wall under the window to listen to him scream frantically.

"That's what she said . . . I don't give a shit who she really was, if she knows, she'll tell." He waited, obviously listening to instructions. "What are we going to do? I knew we wouldn't be able to cover this up . . . You promised the D.A. wouldn't investigate. You said we had money behind us! Naw! I didn't tell her nothin . . . but it don't matter, she knows anyhow."

It was time for me to get a move on. I crept back through the shadows, priding myself on my stalking abilities until I knocked a crate of what must have been bathtub gin off the top of a stack. I didn't turn around to see if anyone was in hot pursuit. I made a dash for the car that would have made Babe Didrickson pea green with envy.

I stomped the starter and wheeled the car out of the gravel parking lot without turning on the headlights. I found the alley and crept between the deserted warehouses through the fog on a hope and a prayer. I thought I heard someone yelling behind me but I didn't stop to chew the fat. Anice stood tensely in my lap peering out into the night like a sailor in a crow's nest looking for land.

A giant man looking like he'd crawled out of a muddy grave stepped out of a shadow and reached for the car. His mouth looked like a hole burned in his face. He moaned in agony. I screamed like a drag queen getting her purse snatched and almost ran the car into the side of a building. I stomped the accelerator, fog or no fog. I was going so fast by the time we went over the railroad tracks that the car rattled like a loaded crap game. Anice and I flew up, I banged my head on the roof of the car hard enough for brain damage and nearly lost control of the car. Anice looked disdainful as she repositioned herself in my lap.

We flew over the bridge on Buffalo Bayou with winged wheels, shot through another warehouse district as dark and scary as an empty purse at a Saks Fifth Avenue half-price sale. I had switched the lights on when I was sure that no one was following me, although they didn't help much and mostly just reflected light back into my eyes from the fog. I kept going until I turned west toward downtown. The blinking colored lights of downtown were as comforting to me as a lighthouse to a sailor home from the sea.

I pulled over in front of a pool hall and slumped back in my seat to catch my breath. A man leaned against the doorway in a trench coat, rolling a toothpick around in his mouth. He grinned and nodded as I sat in the car watching people hurrying by, going to clubs to dance and to beer gardens to drink until they thought they liked themselves. And then they would keep drinking, hoping somebody else would like them, too.

I watched for a while then cranked the car again and backed out into the street. The man in the doorway waved and smiled. I waved back. The feeling was something a bottle couldn't give you. It calmed me down again and I turned the car onto Caroline Street and drifted through the fog toward Susie Noble's house.

I had to park a block away from Susie's house of pleasure since it was Saturday night and the place was swinging. A small jazz band played on the weekends in the bar, a popular spot to be. A lot of people went for the whores, but a lot more went for the music and company. The River Oaks crowd thought it was chic to be there and the women found it titillating. They loved to thrill their friends by mentioning in the most casual and offhand manner that they had been to Susie's with an escort on Saturday night.

A giant bouncer named Tiny, a wide grin on his face, opened the door and leaned over and picked up Anice. "Ah see you got yo guard dog with you tonight, Hollis."

"Yeah. You got a table free for us, Tiny?"

"Ah bet Ah kin get you one real quick like."

"I'll just bet you can, Tiny."

He led me into the bar and handed Anice back to me and went over to a table where two young men in their early thirties were sitting. They looked like they'd been in a fraternity at the University of Texas and never recovered from it. They were in evening clothes with white ties and their sharp little mosquito faces were shiny and clean and terminally shallow.

Tiny leaned over and whispered into their shiny pink ears. Their faces sullied up and they argued with him. Big mistake. He grabbed them by the napes of their necks and rushed them to the bar and plopped them on a pair of stools.

He turned, pulling his coat sleeves back down on his massive arms and straightening his tie. He smiled and motioned me to the table.

As I passed by I heard one of the mosquitoes saying something about what his daddy would do when he heard about "that —" He lowered his voice but I didn't need a clairvoyant to finish it for me. The bartender leaned over and whispered something that made them shut up in a hurry.

I sat down and a waiter brought a bourbon and water, and some water in a bowl for Anice, who was sitting in my lap.

A few minutes passed before Susie appeared in the doorway and crossed to my table and sat down. She looked worried.

"What's going on, Hollis? Lieutenant Brumfield was in here earlier and said Colette had been killed this afternoon. He was fit to be tied, raising hell and threatening people if they didn't talk. Jesus, nobody here knows anything. He threatened to close the place down."

"He's worried. Did he say anything about Darryl Wade?"

"Not specifically. But he did ask if any cops besides Joe came to see Colette."

"What did you tell him?"

"I told him the truth. Darryl Wade came with Joe sometimes and he'd call Colette on the phone now and then. Why?"

I told her what had happened and what I thought it all meant. I was calming down. The whiskey helped. I stayed there until I couldn't put off going to Lily's any longer. I wasn't looking forward to the rest of the evening. I didn't exactly plod out to the car to go to River Oaks, but I didn't skip joyfully, either.

I drove carefully through the cold foggy night, my sense of dread building with every click of the odometer. I cut the lights as I turned into the driveway of the mansion. I don't know why I did, but I did. I guess I had that age-old horror that everyone in the house is hiding behind the draperies peering out at you, laughing and pointing.

At any rate, I banged into the rear end of another car parked in the driveway and had a horrified image of having to turn over every paycheck I ever received for the rest of my life to repair that goddamned Packard. I got the flash out of the glove box to check the damage. There wasn't any, fortunately, and even more fortunately, it wasn't the Packard. It was a maroon '34 Ford and it looked chillingly familiar.

I got back into my car and wiped my face with a Kleenex and patted Anice. "You're going to have to wait in the car, little girl," I said, and cleared my throat to keep my voice from shaking.

I went to the front door and rang the bell. I heard the chimes inside and thought I would faint.

The butler opened the door and announced that Mr. Delacroix had said to show me into the den. I followed him down the hall to the white room one more time. He opened the door and bowed me in. Andrew Delacroix was propped casually against the mantle in a burgundy silk smoking jacket and black trousers. Darryl Wade sat on the white sofa in his rumpled suit.

"Hello, everybody," I said calmly. My voice didn't crack.

"Good evening, Miss Carpenter. So nice of you to come. Mr. Wade and I have been anxiously awaiting your arrival. Funny how things seem to fall into place. My wife will be joining us any moment." He smiled politely. The smile didn't even come close to his eyes.

I looked at Darryl Wade. He grinned tightly at me. I grinned back. We were a happy bunch.

Lily came in and found us grinning like baboons at each other and smiled tentatively, her forehead wrinkled slightly with confusion. She was wearing a black velvet evening dress and was more beautiful than ever. Each time I saw her, I was shocked by her beauty.

"My dear," Delacroix said to her, "meet Sergeant Darryl Wade of the Houston Police Department."

"Hello, Sergeant," she said politely.

"The sergeant is here to arrest your new sweetheart for murder."

It didn't surprise me. Nothing could have surprised me at this point.

Lily laughed for about a split second. Her laughter faded when she saw they weren't kidding. She looked at me, confused.

"Don't worry," I said, smiling reassuringly and holding my left hand up in protestation. The hair on the back of my neck was bristling like a porcupine. "They're joking."

"No, ma'am, we're not joking." Wade's voice grated harshly. He stood up and dug a pair of handcuffs out of his back pocket. "I've got to take her in. She killed two people this week. Thank God we caught her before she killed you, too, ma'am. She's crazy. You never know when these queers are going over the edge. They're sick. I'm going to take her in. She won't bother you again."

Lily looked at me with fear. "What is this all about, Hollis? What is he talking about?"

"Call the police station, Lily. Ask for Frank Brumfield. Tell him to get here as fast as he can. Tell him Wade is here." I didn't take my eyes off Wade as I talked. God, he was a crazy son of a bitch.

Lily headed for the phone, confused but believing me.

"Don't touch that phone." Andrew Delacroix's voice cracked like a whip on a five-hundred-mile cattle drive. "Stay out of this, Lily."

She ignored him and picked up the receiver of the white phone. He crossed to her, snatched the phone out of her hand and yanked the wire out of the wall. Okay, so much for that angle.

Lily covered her mouth with her hand, her eyes wide as she backed away from her husband. "Tell me what you think you are doing, Andrew. You can't seriously think Hollis killed anyone."

"Yes, she did. Don't obstruct the officer, Lily."

"Go to hell, Andrew!"

That was when he hit her. Backhanded her across the mouth. My hand tightened around the .38 in my pocket as I watched her step back from him and sit in the chair, her face filled with pain and astonishment. I considered shooting his dick off, but was afraid I'd miss and hit a vase or something else of value. I'd expected Delacroix to show her what an asshole he really was, but this was more than I'd bargained for.

Wade smiled dangerously. He hadn't even glanced at the side play. His mean little black button eyes were as cold as hub caps in the snow.

"What are you trying to do, Wade? Take me in for two murders you committed? What are you going to do — kill me on the way in and say I was trying to escape? You can't possibly be thinking you can get away with that old wheeze."

He didn't respond. Maybe his smile widened a fraction.

"Frank already knows you did it. He's got an APB out for you right now," I lied.

He stared, unbelieving.

"You don't believe me? Call Susie Noble. Ask her. He was by there earlier asking about you, Wade. Go on — call her. Of course, you'll have to use a phone in another room." My mind was racing, trying to get him out.

I thought I saw his smile diminish almost imperceptibly. Delacroix must have seen it, too.

"Goddammit, Wade! Don't listen to her. Can't you see she's lying? Go on and take her out of here."

"Don't be a sap, Wade," I snapped. "You're already in enough trouble without killing me, too. Do you do everything this rich asshole tells you to do? You can't keep killing everybody who crops up knowing something."

I could see sweat beads on his forehead. I hoped it was from fear and not the fire that was crackling merrily in the fireplace. I wondered how anything so cheerful as a fire could be happening in this room. It was like a singer who kept singing as the audience was being mowed down by a machine gun. Wade had to be under a terrible strain at this point.

"Go on and kill her, you idiot!" Delacroix screamed at him. Something changed in Wade's eyes.

"You like being called an idiot, Sergeant? That's all you'll ever be to him, you know. His idiot. His puppet policeman. Somebody to come in and clean up his dirt, like a maid cleans his toilets," I needled him. "How much did he pay you to steal those guns? I hope it was enough, considering the price you'll have to pay. And those two goofballs he hired to break into my house to look for a story that I wasn't even writing about those goddamn guns. And lo and behold, there was my address book with Joe's name in it. Didn't he call you that night and tell you to bump off Joe? And you, like a good little puppy, went and did it."

I took a breath to see if I would get a response from him. Nothing. Except Andrew Delacroix was looking even cooler and more sophisticated and in control than ever. Lily sat in the chair watching. Every now and then a tear rolled slowly down her cheek.

"Maybe you were happy to bump off Joe — that way you would have Colette to yourself. And Joe's share of the take, let's don't forget that. But you've got to miss Joe. Right? He was, after all, a good friend of yours." I laughed softly.

Wade said, "For your information, nobody had to tell me to kill Joe — he was going to squeal. His conscience got the best of him in the end." He sneered and reached under his coat and pulled a .45 out of the shoulder holster and aimed it at me.

Now it was Andrew Delacroix's turn to laugh softly. The barrel of the gun looked like a pipe on an oil line. I felt achy all over like I had the flu. I thought about sitting down. He would have a hard time explaining how an escaping murder suspect came to be sitting down when he had to shoot. But then I wouldn't be able to get my pistol out of my pocket fast enough. Come to think of it, I probably wouldn't be able to standing up, either, but I kept on standing just in case. I shifted all of my weight to my left leg since my knee was hurting. Wade cocked the gun when I moved.

"Let's get going," he growled. "I don't even care whether they believe me or not, I'll get a great deal of pleasure out of killing you, anyhow."

Lily sobbed softly. I appreciated the vote of confidence.

"Wait a minute, Wade," I whined, hating myself

for doing it, but I could see he enjoyed it and it made him relax a bit. Good. "I just want to know a few more answers before we leave."

He didn't say anything, but he didn't move toward me, either. I hoped he wouldn't wonder why I was keeping my hands in my pockets when it was warm in the room. But, then again, he wouldn't be expecting me to bring a gun on a social call, either.

"Colette figured out you killed Joe and either said something to you, or you overheard her on the phone talking to me, or you could just tell by the way she was acting that she knew something. So you killed her. Okay."

"Actually, I saw your card on the cocktail table and knew she was up to something. I asked her about it and she started sniveling and lying — I hate a lying sniveler."

"I guess you must, you beat her brains out. Remind me not to snivel." I grinned at Andrew Delacroix. "Just to get all the facts straight, you had the guns stolen to ship to Bolivia, right? I finally figured that one out. Took me a while since I'm slightly retarded. There was a picture in the paper the other day of Joe Allard, the head of Curtiss Wright Aircraft Corporation, being indicted in New York for smuggling guns to Bolivia. Never mind that Congress passed a neutrality law against getting involved in the boundary war between Bolivia and Paraguay. You rich boys are above the law, aren't you, Delacroix? What the hell makes you think you're so special?"

He shrugged and smiled mockingly. "I don't think I'm special — it's just that sometimes it's necessary to break stupid laws passed by an ignorant

Congress. Our legislators sometimes don't know what's best for our country and its allies. Bolivia needs our help — I happen to be an honorary colonel in the Bolivian army, Miss Carpenter."

"Are you shitting me?" I screamed. "All this because the poor little rich boy wants to play army? I should have known you were crazy when I saw your war room over there. Lily said your daddy left that shit to you. What the hell goes on in this house — you're playing army and having people killed to please your dead father, and Lily married a sadistic lunatic to please her mother. Too bad I'm going to be killed and won't be able to check into what really happened to Lily's first husband. I wonder where you were the night he was killed. I guess it doesn't really matter, though. There are definitely three people dead now because of you!"

Wade looked confused, then.

"Oh, sure, Wade. Didn't you hear about Cotton Peeples — the stupid little rum-dum. You didn't have anything to do with that one, did you Wade?" I turned back to Delacroix, who lifted his eyebrows in a bored fashion. Nothing fazed him.

"That really confused me, Mr. Delacroix. For a while there, I was thinking Cotton was trying to kill me. Goes to show how self-centered I am. Took me a while to figure out he was after your wife. I kept wondering how he could possibly have known I was going to be at the Rice Hotel. He didn't. But he knew your wife was going to be there. She told me herself she goes every Friday night. So you tried to have her killed. Why? For her money? Or were you just tired of living with someone who didn't love you? Why didn't you just get a divorce, you crazy asshole? It was the money, wasn't it? You want her money, too — probably to help finance your army. It's probably hard to support a war on your piddling old fortune — you needed hers, too. I'll bet you were mighty surprised to come home and find her still alive."

Lily was staring at her lap, crying silently.

"I don't know what you're talking about," Delacroix said quietly.

"Sure you do! Are you going to kill her and blame that one on me — the jealous lesbian — or maybe you'll blame Wade here — the lunatic killer cop. That's it. One way or the other you plan on the three of us being dead in a very short while. A real blood bath with you the only one left standing. Jesus H. Christ! You really are crazy, to think you can get away with it." I began to guffaw loudly, hoping to unnerve him. It worked better than I had intended.

"Kill her. Go on and shoot!" he screamed hysterically at Wade.

Boy, when those cool ones crack, they crack big time. Just goes to show how they're barely hanging on by a thread.

Wade stared at Delacroix, his mouth slightly open. I think he had believed some of what I had been blabbing.

"Go on and shoot, you dumb son of a bitch!"

He shouldn't have done that. Wade's mouth closed and a flush of red began to creep up his neck toward his face like a hunter stalking a deer.

"Didn't you hear me? Kill her." He lunged at Wade, grabbing for the pistol. Wade looked confused and put his left arm up to block Delacroix. Delacroix hit the arm and Wade fired point blank into Delacroix's stomach. I pulled my pistol out and yelled at Wade to drop his gun. He turned toward me savagely. I fired and prayed. He grunted and his hand dropped, then came up again to aim at me. I fired again, then again. He dropped the gun and fell against the wall and slid slowly down it. He was dead before he hit the floor.

Lily's mouth was open and she seemed to be screaming silently. The butler crashed through the door and I yelled at him to take her out of the room. I didn't seem to be able to say anything in a normal tone of voice; every time I opened my mouth, a yell came out. He grabbed her without a question and took her from the den. Delacroix was still standing, clutching his stomach and staring down at the blood oozing between his fingers. His mouth opened and closed and he looked at me with horror and confusion.

I walked over to him and helped him over to a chair. "Not quite the way you figured it would turn out, huh, Mr. Delacroix?"

I was tired. The room wasn't so white anymore. I felt dizzy from looking at the blood, and sat on the couch. I looked at the gun in my hand and threw it down beside me. I had never shot anybody before.

Delacroix was making noises in his throat. I wanted to leave the room to get away from him. But his eyes were pleading for me to stay. He was scared.

I waited there until the police and an ambulance arrived. They took Delacroix to the Richmond

Hospital Clinic. He died a few hours later on the operating table. That was good. It simplified things.

I called Gael and Katherine. They stayed with me while I talked to the police. I was up all night explaining over and over until they were satisfied. They believed me, all right, they just wanted to keep me up to give me a hard time. Lily's doctor had come over and given her something to help her sleep. Katherine took charge and called Lily's parents and stayed with her while Gael and I dealt with the press.

I didn't get home to bed until ten o'clock the next morning and Anice was as exhausted as I was. I woke up that afternoon feeling like a decomposing corpse. I took a shower and got dressed for Joe's funeral. Gael came by and drove me to the funeral and to the cemetery afterwards. I had already cried for Joe and now I was mad at him. I supposed that sooner or later I would forgive him and let him go.

Gael and Katherine went to Delacroix's funeral as my representatives. I figured my presence would have been about as tasteful as camel dung in a crystal punch bowl as far as Lily's friends and family were concerned.

I got a call from Lily the afternoon of Andrew's funeral saying that her mother had thought it would be a good idea for her to get out of town for a while and had made reservations on a plane for Mexico that evening. Her parents owned a villa outside Mexico City and they'd go there for a while, then possibly to Europe. She needed to get her thoughts together about everything that had happened. I said I understood.

I did understand. I was the bearer of bad news — the one the Greeks used to kill off. I had brought blood and ugliness into her life and I was being killed off emotionally.

Frank Brumfield called the next day and said that the bullets fired from Wade's gun matched the bullet that killed Joe. He also said they found the billy club in the trunk of Wade's car that had been used to kill Colette.

Anice and I pretty much went to the dogs for the next couple of weeks. We shuffled pitifully around the house living mainly on chocolate pie and brownies. I didn't wear anything but a bathrobe the entire time and Anice's beard got matted and unruly. I don't know what I looked like because I didn't look in the mirror — I was crazy, but I wasn't that crazy.

I read in the newspaper that the guns stolen from the evidence room were recovered when the ship transporting them docked in South America. An investigation was underway in Washington of certain United States representatives who were probably in on the scheme with Delacroix — so that accounted for the trips to Washington and the limo that had picked him up at the airport. Good — that had been bothering me — now I could die happy.

After about two and a half weeks, I got dressed and Anice and I crawled out to the car and headed south on Woodhead to South Boulevard to Bill Oswald's house.

The cowboy torpedo showed me into Bill's office without announcing me. I guess he had special instructions.

Bill hugged me, then picked up Anice and hugged her. "You look like shit," he said gallantly.

"I feel like shit."

"Why don't you sit down and tell me about it."

So I sat down and told him about Lily. He nodded and grunted appropriate responses and fed me a wonderful lunch, which I gobbled down in spite of being brokenhearted. Anice ate even faster than I did and burped loudly when she finished.

I came to the purpose of my visit. "Doesn't one of your goons drive a green Chevrolet, Bill?"

"I think so — why?"

"Did you have a couple of your 'ranchhands' following me around to protect me?"

"You have such a vivid imagination, Hollis." He chuckled and sipped his wine.

"You should tell that to Cotton Peeples."

"Who in the world is Cotton Peeples?"

"The creep that was mowed down in front of the Rice Hotel a few weeks ago by a goon or goons unknown."

"Oh, yes. I believe I remember reading about that in the paper."

"I'll bet you did. Did you also read about Tully Kirk getting the shit beaten out of him by somebody in a cowboy outfit? Did you send one of your goons up there to persuade him to cooperate with me, Bill?"

"Now, really, Hollis!" He was highly indignant, which meant I was right about that, too.

"Bill, I have told you before that I can take care of myself."

He grinned. "Did I ever tell you you're just like a daughter to me, Hollis?"

I shook my head and grinned. "I guess I'll go home now. I'm tired."

I wrapped Bill's dessert in a napkin to take with me and gathered Anice up and went home.

The phone was ringing as we slouched back into the house. I answered it without interest.

"Hollis?"

"Yes?"

"This is Lily," she explained unnecessarily.

My heart was pounding like a sledgehammer. "Yes."

"I got homesick."

"You did? Where are you?"

"I'm at Grand Central Station. Would it be too much of an imposition to ask you to pick me up?"

"Would that be Grand Central in New York or Grand Central in Houston?"

"In Houston, silly," she laughed.

"Right now?" I asked.

"Whenever you can get here."

"That squealing you hear outside is my car pulling up out front."

She laughed again.

"I love you."

"I love you, too."

A few of the publications of

THE NAIAD PRESS, INC.

P.O. Box 10543 • Tallahassee, Florida 32302

Phone (904) 539-5965

Mail orders welcome. Please include 15% postage.

TOUCHWOOD by Karin Kallmaker. 240 pp. Loving, May/December romance.	ISBN 0-941483-76-2	$8.95
BAYOU CITY SECRETS by Deborah Powell. 224 pp. A Hollis Carpenter mystery. First in a series.	ISBN 0-941483-91-6	8.95
COP OUT by Claire McNab. 208 pp. 4th Det. Insp. Carol Ashton mystery.	ISBN 0-941483-84-3	8.95
LODESTAR by Phyllis Horn. 224 pp. Romantic, fast-moving adventure.	ISBN 0-941483-83-5	8.95
THE BEVERLY MALIBU by Katherine V. Forrest. 288 pp. A Kate Delafield Mystery. 3rd in a series. (HC)	ISBN 0-941483-47-9	16.95
Paperback	ISBN 0-941483-48-7	9.95
THAT OLD STUDEBAKER by Lee Lynch. 272 pp. Andy's affair with Regina and her attachment to her beloved car.	ISBN 0-941483-82-7	9.95
PASSION'S LEGACY by Lori Paige. 224 pp. Sarah is swept into the arms of Augusta Pym in this delightful historical romance.	ISBN 0-941483-81-9	8.95
THE PROVIDENCE FILE by Amanda Kyle Williams. 256 pp. Second espionage thriller featuring lesbian agent Madison McGuire	ISBN 0-941483-92-4	8.95
I LEFT MY HEART by Jaye Maiman. 320 pp. A Robin Miller Mystery. First in a series.	ISBN 0-941483-72-X	9.95
THE PRICE OF SALT by Patricia Highsmith (writing as Claire Morgan). 288 pp. Classic lesbian novel, first issued in 1952 . . . acknowledged by its author under her own, very famous, name.	ISBN 1-56280-003-5	8.95
SIDE BY SIDE by Isabel Miller. 256 pp. From beloved author of *Patience and Sarah.*	ISBN 0-941483-77-0	8.95
SOUTHBOUND by Sheila Ortiz Taylor. 240 pp. Hilarious sequel to *Faultline.*	ISBN 0-941483-78-9	8.95
STAYING POWER: LONG TERM LESBIAN COUPLES by Susan E. Johnson. 352 pp. Joys of coupledom.	ISBN 0-941-483-75-4	12.95
SLICK by Camarin Grae. 304 pp. Exotic, erotic adventure.	ISBN 0-941483-74-6	9.95

NINTH LIFE by Lauren Wright Douglas. 256 pp. A Caitlin Reece mystery. 2nd in a series.	ISBN 0-941483-50-9	8.95
PLAYERS by Robbi Sommers. 192 pp. Sizzling, erotic novel.	ISBN 0-941483-73-8	8.95
MURDER AT RED ROOK RANCH by Dorothy Tell. 224 pp. First Poppy Dillworth adventure.	ISBN 0-941483-80-0	8.95
LESBIAN SURVIVAL MANUAL by Rhonda Dicksion. 112 pp. Cartoons!	ISBN 0-941483-71-1	8.95
A ROOM FULL OF WOMEN by Elisabeth Nonas. 256 pp. Contemporary Lesbian lives.	ISBN 0-941483-69-X	8.95
MURDER IS RELATIVE by Karen Saum. 256 pp. The first Brigid Donovan mystery.	ISBN 0-941483-70-3	8.95
PRIORITIES by Lynda Lyons 288 pp. Science fiction with a twist.	ISBN 0-941483-66-5	8.95
THEME FOR DIVERSE INSTRUMENTS by Jane Rule. 208 pp. Powerful romantic lesbian stories.	ISBN 0-941483-63-0	8.95
LESBIAN QUERIES by Hertz & Ertman. 112 pp. The questions you were too embarrassed to ask.	ISBN 0-941483-67-3	8.95
CLUB 12 by Amanda Kyle Williams. 288 pp. Espionage thriller featuring a lesbian agent!	ISBN 0-941483-64-9	8.95
DEATH DOWN UNDER by Claire McNab. 240 pp. 3rd Det. Insp. Carol Ashton mystery.	ISBN 0-941483-39-8	8.95
MONTANA FEATHERS by Penny Hayes. 256 pp. Vivian and Elizabeth find love in frontier Montana.	ISBN 0-941483-61-4	8.95
CHESAPEAKE PROJECT by Phyllis Horn. 304 pp. Jessie & Meredith in perilous adventure.	ISBN 0-941483-58-4	8.95
LIFESTYLES by Jackie Calhoun. 224 pp. Contemporary Lesbian lives and loves.	ISBN 0-941483-57-6	8.95
VIRAGO by Karen Marie Christa Minns. 208 pp. Darsen has chosen Ginny.	ISBN 0-941483-56-8	8.95
WILDERNESS TREK by Dorothy Tell. 192 pp. Six women on vacation learning "new" skills.	ISBN 0-941483-60-6	8.95
MURDER BY THE BOOK by Pat Welch. 256 pp. A Helen Black Mystery. First in a series.	ISBN 0-941483-59-2	8.95
BERRIGAN by Vicki P. McConnell. 176 pp. Youthful Lesbian — romantic, idealistic Berrigan.	ISBN 0-941483-55-X	8.95
LESBIANS IN GERMANY by Lillian Faderman & B. Eriksson. 128 pp. Fiction, poetry, essays.	ISBN 0-941483-62-2	8.95
THERE'S SOMETHING I'VE BEEN MEANING TO TELL YOU Ed. by Loralee MacPike. 288 pp. Gay men and lesbians coming out to their children.	ISBN 0-941483-44-4	9.95
	ISBN 0-941483-54-1	16.95

LIFTING BELLY by Gertrude Stein. Ed. by Rebecca Mark. 104 pp. Erotic poetry.	ISBN 0-941483-51-7	8.95
	ISBN 0-941483-53-3	14.95
ROSE PENSKI by Roz Perry. 192 pp. Adult lovers in a long-term relationship.	ISBN 0-941483-37-1	8.95
AFTER THE FIRE by Jane Rule. 256 pp. Warm, human novel by this incomparable author.	ISBN 0-941483-45-2	8.95
SUE SLATE, PRIVATE EYE by Lee Lynch. 176 pp. The gay folk of Peacock Alley are *all cats*.	ISBN 0-941483-52-5	8.95
CHRIS by Randy Salem. 224 pp. Golden oldie. Handsome Chris and her adventures.	ISBN 0-941483-42-8	8.95
THREE WOMEN by March Hastings. 232 pp. Golden oldie. A triangle among wealthy sophisticates.	ISBN 0-941483-43-6	8.95
RICE AND BEANS by Valeria Taylor. 232 pp. Love and romance on poverty row.	ISBN 0-941483-41-X	8.95
PLEASURES by Robbi Sommers. 204 pp. Unprecedented eroticism.	ISBN 0-941483-49-5	8.95
EDGEWISE by Camarin Grae. 372 pp. Spellbinding adventure.	ISBN 0-941483-19-3	9.95
FATAL REUNION by Claire McNab. 224 pp. 2nd Det. Inspec. Carol Ashton mystery.	ISBN 0-941483-40-1	8.95
KEEP TO ME STRANGER by Sarah Aldridge. 372 pp. Romance set in a department store dynasty.	ISBN 0-941483-38-X	9.95
HEARTSCAPE by Sue Gambill. 204 pp. American lesbian in Portugal.	ISBN 0-941483-33-9	8.95
IN THE BLOOD by Lauren Wright Douglas. 252 pp. Lesbian science fiction adventure fantasy	ISBN 0-941483-22-3	8.95
THE BEE'S KISS by Shirley Verel. 216 pp. Delicate, delicious romance.	ISBN 0-941483-36-3	8.95
RAGING MOTHER MOUNTAIN by Pat Emmerson. 264 pp. Furosa Firechild's adventures in Wonderland.	ISBN 0-941483-35-5	8.95
IN EVERY PORT by Karin Kallmaker. 228 pp. Jessica's sexy, adventuresome travels.	ISBN 0-941483-37-7	8.95
OF LOVE AND GLORY by Evelyn Kennedy. 192 pp. Exciting WWII romance.	ISBN 0-941483-32-0	8.95
CLICKING STONES by Nancy Tyler Glenn. 288 pp. Love transcending time.	ISBN 0-941483-31-2	8.95
SURVIVING SISTERS by Gail Pass. 252 pp. Powerful love story.	ISBN 0-941483-16-9	8.95
SOUTH OF THE LINE by Catherine Ennis. 216 pp. Civil War adventure.	ISBN 0-941483-29-0	8.95

WOMAN PLUS WOMAN by Dolores Klaich. 300 pp. Supurb Lesbian overview. ISBN 0-941483-28-2 9.95

SLOW DANCING AT MISS POLLY'S by Sheila Ortiz Taylor. 96 pp. Lesbian Poetry ISBN 0-941483-30-4 7.95

DOUBLE DAUGHTER by Vicki P. McConnell. 216 pp. A Nyla Wade Mystery, third in the series. ISBN 0-941483-26-6 8.95

HEAVY GILT by Delores Klaich. 192 pp. Lesbian detective/ disappearing homophobes/upper class gay society. ISBN 0-941483-25-8 8.95

THE FINER GRAIN by Denise Ohio. 216 pp. Brilliant young college lesbian novel. ISBN 0-941483-11-8 8.95

THE AMAZON TRAIL by Lee Lynch. 216 pp. Life, travel & lore of famous lesbian author. ISBN 0-941483-27-4 8.95

HIGH CONTRAST by Jessie Lattimore. 264 pp. Women of the Crystal Palace. ISBN 0-941483-17-7 8.95

OCTOBER OBSESSION by Meredith More. Josie's rich, secret Lesbian life. ISBN 0-941483-18-5 8.95

LESBIAN CROSSROADS by Ruth Baetz. 276 pp. Contemporary Lesbian lives. ISBN 0-941483-21-5 9.95

BEFORE STONEWALL: THE MAKING OF A GAY AND LESBIAN COMMUNITY by Andrea Weiss & Greta Schiller. 96 pp., 25 illus. ISBN 0-941483-20-7 7.95

WE WALK THE BACK OF THE TIGER by Patricia A. Murphy. 192 pp. Romantic Lesbian novel/beginning women's movement. ISBN 0-941483-13-4 8.95

SUNDAY'S CHILD by Joyce Bright. 216 pp. Lesbian athletics, at last the novel about sports. ISBN 0-941483-12-6 8.95

OSTEN'S BAY by Zenobia N. Vole. 204 pp. Sizzling adventure romance set on Bonaire. ISBN 0-941483-15-0 8.95

LESSONS IN MURDER by Claire McNab. 216 pp. 1st Det. Inspec. Carol Ashton mystery — erotic tension!. ISBN 0-941483-14-2 8.95

YELLOWTHROAT by Penny Hayes. 240 pp. Margarita, bandit, kidnaps Julia. ISBN 0-941483-10-X 8.95

SAPPHISTRY: THE BOOK OF LESBIAN SEXUALITY by Pat Califia. 3d edition, revised. 208 pp. ISBN 0-941483-24-X 8.95

CHERISHED LOVE by Evelyn Kennedy. 192 pp. Erotic Lesbian love story. ISBN 0-941483-08-8 8.95

LAST SEPTEMBER by Helen R. Hull. 208 pp. Six stories & a glorious novella. ISBN 0-941483-09-6 8.95

THE SECRET IN THE BIRD by Camarin Grae. 312 pp. Striking, psychological suspense novel. ISBN 0-941483-05-3 8.95

TO THE LIGHTNING by Catherine Ennis. 208 pp. Romantic Lesbian 'Robinson Crusoe' adventure. ISBN 0-941483-06-1 8.95

THE OTHER SIDE OF VENUS by Shirley Verel. 224 pp. Luminous, romantic love story. ISBN 0-941483-07-X 8.95

DREAMS AND SWORDS by Katherine V. Forrest. 192 pp. Romantic, erotic, imaginative stories. ISBN 0-941483-03-7 8.95

MEMORY BOARD by Jane Rule. 336 pp. Memorable novel about an aging Lesbian couple. ISBN 0-941483-02-9 9.95

THE ALWAYS ANONYMOUS BEAST by Lauren Wright Douglas. 224 pp. A Caitlin Reece mystery. First in a series. ISBN 0-941483-04-5 8.95

SEARCHING FOR SPRING by Patricia A. Murphy. 224 pp. Novel about the recovery of love. ISBN 0-941483-00-2 8.95

DUSTY'S QUEEN OF HEARTS DINER by Lee Lynch. 240 pp. Romantic blue-collar novel. ISBN 0-941483-01-0 8.95

PARENTS MATTER by Ann Muller. 240 pp. Parents' relationships with Lesbian daughters and gay sons. ISBN 0-930044-91-6 9.95

THE PEARLS by Shelley Smith. 176 pp. Passion and fun in the Caribbean sun. ISBN 0-930044-93-2 7.95

MAGDALENA by Sarah Aldridge. 352 pp. Epic Lesbian novel set on three continents. ISBN 0-930044-99-1 8.95

THE BLACK AND WHITE OF IT by Ann Allen Shockley. 144 pp. Short stories. ISBN 0-930044-96-7 7.95

SAY JESUS AND COME TO ME by Ann Allen Shockley. 288 pp. Contemporary romance. ISBN 0-930044-98-3 8.95

LOVING HER by Ann Allen Shockley. 192 pp. Romantic love story. ISBN 0-930044-97-5 7.95

MURDER AT THE NIGHTWOOD BAR by Katherine V. Forrest. 240 pp. A Kate Delafield mystery. Second in a series. ISBN 0-930044-92-4 8.95

ZOE'S BOOK by Gail Pass. 224 pp. Passionate, obsessive love story. ISBN 0-930044-95-9 7.95

WINGED DANCER by Camarin Grae. 228 pp. Erotic Lesbian adventure story. ISBN 0-930044-88-6 8.95

PAZ by Camarin Grae. 336 pp. Romantic Lesbian adventurer with the power to change the world. ISBN 0-930044-89-4 8.95

SOUL SNATCHER by Camarin Grae. 224 pp. A puzzle, an adventure, a mystery — Lesbian romance. ISBN 0-930044-90-8 8.95

THE LOVE OF GOOD WOMEN by Isabel Miller. 224 pp. Long-awaited new novel by the author of the beloved *Patience and Sarah.* ISBN 0-930044-81-9 8.95

THE HOUSE AT PELHAM FALLS by Brenda Weathers. 240 pp. Suspenseful Lesbian ghost story.	ISBN 0-930044-79-7	7.95
HOME IN YOUR HANDS by Lee Lynch. 240 pp. More stories from the author of *Old Dyke Tales.*	ISBN 0-930044-80-0	7.95
EACH HAND A MAP by Anita Skeen. 112 pp. Real-life poems that touch us all.	ISBN 0-930044-82-7	6.95
SURPLUS by Sylvia Stevenson. 342 pp. A classic early Lesbian novel.	ISBN 0-930044-78-9	7.95
PEMBROKE PARK by Michelle Martin. 256 pp. Derring-do and daring romance in Regency England.	ISBN 0-930044-77-0	7.95
THE LONG TRAIL by Penny Hayes. 248 pp. Vivid adventures of two women in love in the old west.	ISBN 0-930044-76-2	8.95
HORIZON OF THE HEART by Shelley Smith. 192 pp. Hot romance in summertime New England.	ISBN 0-930044-75-4	7.95
AN EMERGENCE OF GREEN by Katherine V. Forrest. 288 pp. Powerful novel of sexual discovery.	ISBN 0-930044-69-X	8.95
THE LESBIAN PERIODICALS INDEX edited by Claire Potter. 432 pp. Author & subject index.	ISBN 0-930044-74-6	29.95
DESERT OF THE HEART by Jane Rule. 224 pp. A classic; basis for the movie *Desert Hearts.*	ISBN 0-930044-73-8	8.95
SPRING FORWARD/FALL BACK by Sheila Ortiz Taylor. 288 pp. Literary novel of timeless love.	ISBN 0-930044-70-3	7.95
FOR KEEPS by Elisabeth Nonas. 144 pp. Contemporary novel about losing and finding love.	ISBN 0-930044-71-1	7.95
TORCHLIGHT TO VALHALLA by Gale Wilhelm. 128 pp. Classic novel by a great Lesbian writer.	ISBN 0-930044-68-1	7.95
LESBIAN NUNS: BREAKING SILENCE edited by Rosemary Curb and Nancy Manahan. 432 pp. Unprecedented autobiographies of religious life.	ISBN 0-930044-62-2	9.95
THE SWASHBUCKLER by Lee Lynch. 288 pp. Colorful novel set in Greenwich Village in the sixties.	ISBN 0-930044-66-5	8.95
MISFORTUNE'S FRIEND by Sarah Aldridge. 320 pp. Historical Lesbian novel set on two continents.	ISBN 0-930044-67-3	7.95
A STUDIO OF ONE'S OWN by Ann Stokes. Edited by Dolores Klaich. 128 pp. Autobiography.	ISBN 0-930044-64-9	7.95
SEX VARIANT WOMEN IN LITERATURE by Jeannette Howard Foster. 448 pp. Literary history.	ISBN 0-930044-65-7	8.95
A HOT-EYED MODERATE by Jane Rule. 252 pp. Hard-hitting essays on gay life; writing; art.	ISBN 0-930044-57-6	7.95
INLAND PASSAGE AND OTHER STORIES by Jane Rule. 288 pp. Wide-ranging new collection.	ISBN 0-930044-56-8	7.95

WE TOO ARE DRIFTING by Gale Wilhelm. 128 pp. Timeless Lesbian novel, a masterpiece.	ISBN 0-930044-61-4	6.95
AMATEUR CITY by Katherine V. Forrest. 224 pp. A Kate Delafield mystery. First in a series.	ISBN 0-930044-55-X	8.95
THE SOPHIE HOROWITZ STORY by Sarah Schulman. 176 pp. Engaging novel of madcap intrigue.	ISBN 0-930044-54-1	7.95
THE BURNTON WIDOWS by Vickie P. McConnell. 272 pp. A Nyla Wade mystery, second in the series.	ISBN 0-930044-52-5	7.95
OLD DYKE TALES by Lee Lynch. 224 pp. Extraordinary stories of our diverse Lesbian lives.	ISBN 0-930044-51-7	8.95
DAUGHTERS OF A CORAL DAWN by Katherine V. Forrest. 240 pp. Novel set in a Lesbian new world.	ISBN 0-930044-50-9	8.95
AGAINST THE SEASON by Jane Rule. 224 pp. Luminous, complex novel of interrelationships.	ISBN 0-930044-48-7	8.95
LOVERS IN THE PRESENT AFTERNOON by Kathleen Fleming. 288 pp. A novel about recovery and growth.	ISBN 0-930044-46-0	8.95
TOOTHPICK HOUSE by Lee Lynch. 264 pp. Love between two Lesbians of different classes.	ISBN 0-930044-45-2	7.95
MADAME AURORA by Sarah Aldridge. 256 pp. Historical novel featuring a charismatic "seer."	ISBN 0-930044-44-4	7.95
CURIOUS WINE by Katherine V. Forrest. 176 pp. Passionate Lesbian love story, a best-seller.	ISBN 0-930044-43-6	8.95
BLACK LESBIAN IN WHITE AMERICA by Anita Cornwell. 141 pp. Stories, essays, autobiography.	ISBN 0-930044-41-X	7.95
CONTRACT WITH THE WORLD by Jane Rule. 340 pp. Powerful, panoramic novel of gay life.	ISBN 0-930044-28-2	9.95
MRS. PORTER'S LETTER by Vicki P. McConnell. 224 pp. The first Nyla Wade mystery.	ISBN 0-930044-29-0	7.95
TO THE CLEVELAND STATION by Carol Anne Douglas. 192 pp. Interracial Lesbian love story.	ISBN 0-930044-27-4	6.95
THE NESTING PLACE by Sarah Aldridge. 224 pp. A three-woman triangle — love conquers all!	ISBN 0-930044-26-6	7.95
THIS IS NOT FOR YOU by Jane Rule. 284 pp. A letter to a beloved is also an intricate novel.	ISBN 0-930044-25-8	8.95
FAULTLINE by Sheila Ortiz Taylor. 140 pp. Warm, funny, literate story of a startling family.	ISBN 0-930044-24-X	6.95
THE LESBIAN IN LITERATURE by Barbara Grier. 3d ed. Foreword by Maida Tilchen. 240 pp. Comprehensive bibliography. Literary ratings; rare photos.	ISBN 0-930044-23-1	7.95
ANNA'S COUNTRY by Elizabeth Lang. 208 pp. A woman finds her Lesbian identity.	ISBN 0-930044-19-3	8.95